The Council:

A Few Came Together to Become the Manifestation of JUSTICE.

Charles L. Price II

Printed in The United States of America

First Edition

www.councilseries.com

Development Editor:
Khloe Cain, *Khloe's Thoughts Editing*
Amber M. Price
Avan D. Price

Line Editor:
Khloe Cain, *Khloe's Thoughts Editing*

Copy Editor & Proof Editor:
Florence D. Cuffee
Amber M. Price

Cover Design:
Charles L. Price II
Cat Gilray

Cover Art & Typography:
Cat Gilray

DEDICATION

To God:
Thank you for bringing me through all my rejections, turmoils, battles of racism, resentment for life, resentment for people, and resentment for myself. In the dark times I have faced where I almost gave up on life, you've held my hand to show me there is a divine purpose for me to live, endure, and produce to make this world better.
Since my resurgence, I have grown in every way possible. I know who I am in You, and with You, all things are possible.
Thank You.

To My Wife:
Thank you for being my Sunshine! You are more than what I was hoping to find in a wife. You have given my life stability, peace, responsibility, and comfort that very few will have or embrace. I'm glad you deemed me worthy of your respect, honor, and submission. I pray that you know I will give nothing less than all of me to make you proud to say, "That's my husband."   #Happy Spouse. Happy House.

To My Family:
Thank you for the endless love. Thank you for the tests. Thank you for the infinite memories. Thank you for the laughs. Thank you for being my foundation. Thank you for your protection.

Mom & Dad, I know your childhoods weren't the best, so I thank you for loving me and giving me all that you had just so I could say, "I am loved." I WILL make you proud.

To My Tribe:
Rather you scarred me or loved me. Rather you helped me or harmed me. Thank you for your contribution to my life.

To those I consider family and have played a vital role in my life and development. I'm grateful you've been placed in my life! You chose to learn of me and give me the highest honor possible, being my friend. You all have done the best thing ever, and that's loving me through all my faults. You've told me the truth even when it hurt. You've pushed me, embraced me, and respected me despite differences. I truly love you all! You already know, rather it's been ten minutes or three years since we've talked, you call, Charles is on the way!   Fellas, #DCMoment

To Javier:
Words can never describe what your friendship and brotherhood meant to me. Even though we were young, the lessons you taught me are etched in stone on my heart. I pray you are in God's hands and at peace. I promised you at your bedside, I will never forget you. I pray you are proud of me and know that I am always your friend. You, me, and Henry will always remain the Bicycle Gang!

To the Reader:
Life is hard. It has highs and lows. The sign of greatness is your impact and your endurance. Don't hide from life's difficulties but build the strength necessary to be more than a conqueror of life.

<u>You got this!</u>

I hope you enjoy this novel!

CONTENTS

1

DENMARK VESEY MANIFESTO - JUNE 15, 1822

The rocking of the seas is still wit' me...

My family's warmth is still wit' me...

The terrible sights I've been a witness to are wit' me...

I can never forget these things, for they have directed me on this path and to build these last moments.

I pray that these writings make it into the hands of a loving person. One who will feel the pain behind these words. One who will understand the actions that follow these words. Even my secret ability to pen these thoughts can cost me what fraction of a life I have left. The stolen life I've lived 'till now. My brethren and I are not stealing but merely reclaiming what they took from us. America's Pharaohs will no more keep us in bondage, for if I am to be my peoples' Moses, I pray that the Lord will be on our side in these *upcoming days. They told me $600 would buy my freedom, and I paid my debt. Yet I've learned purchased freedom for a nigger is yet conditional. I was not given the ability to buy my family's freedom, for I would have gladly given ten times ova' to purchase them freedom. Yet, are the decisions or requests of livestock ever honored? The decision to be slaughtered or to live is granted at the hand of the owner.*

My family's warmth is forever wit' me.

Please give me the strength to lead the brethren to claim our true freedom. We've earned it. If victory is given to our captors Lord, allow these writings to help another to make victory.

SECTION 1

2

OFF TO A GREAT START - NOVEMBER 18, 2016

"Vanessa!"

"Vanessa Whitfield, we go through this every mornin'! If you don't get up out that bed!"

Every morning begins with Mom shouting through the house. The only thing worse than the yelling is the loud footsteps and the unavoidable gust of chill air coming from my door being whipped open.

"Vanessa! Girl, I know you hear me!" Mom says. "You like all dis yellin' in the morning," Mom said through a pleasant smile and tone. Mom secretly loves this process. I secretly love it too. I begrudgingly whip the blankets off of my head, so I can slowly rise and greet her with my best zombie impersonation.

"Good morning, Mother. How are you this wonderful morning?"

"I'd be better if you would get up on ya' own. You're too old for these wake up calls. I'mma let you sleep and miss ya' bus, then it's going to be a discussion you have with your dad. Now get going; you got about thirty minutes before the bus gets here."

As she exits abruptly out of my room to go back downstairs, she slows down just enough to make a pitstop at Eddie's room, jingling the door handle to find it's locked.

"Eddie, you get up too! And I'm not playing! And why is this door locked? You lock doors on ones you own."

"Get up!" she proclaims as she makes her way down the stairs. Accompanying her pitter-patter of feet on the stairs, I hear Eddie work up a muffled, "Yeah, yeah."

Another day. Another emotionless day filled with school. Oh, how I love the bland prison walls, the ominous hallways filled with lockers, and bored teachers with the tall task of teaching kids where their primary goal is to escape their clutches. Thankfully, it's the last Friday until winter break. I need to get through today first.

I jump out of bed to slam my door and take a deep breath. I scan my room and think to myself, *let's see if I can get ready to make it to school on time.*

As I make my way down the stairs, I take a hard left to stroll into the kitchen where Mom announces, "With five minutes to spare, ladies and gentlemen, she's ready to go."

Naturally, I take a large bow towards my audience in recognizing my feat of an excellent morning performance. Mom chuckles into her coffee as she nurses it for her morning rituals. Mom likes to start her mornings with CNN and coffee. Somehow, getting a healthy dose of caffeine and capturing the day's political unrest makes for an easier day at work. As she would put it, it is a force of evil we have to be aware of because their decisions and actions affect us whether we like it or not.

After listening to political pundits argue, like my brother and I over the choice of movie for movie night for a few seconds, I start scouring the cabinets for a container to pour some Cheerios. I rummage through the cabinets for a good six seconds before I shout for mom's assistance to help me find the top half of this container.

"Hey, Mom, where are all the lids?"

Too focused on her dose of news and coffee, she sarcastically replies, "…in the cabinet with the rest of them."

Matching her wits, I said, "Yes, Mom, I found the bottom, but I can't find the matching top."

"Well, sounds like the *Borrowers* took it."

That's her response to everything we can't find in this house. When you live in a house with a spoiled baby brother that's gifted with intelligence, things such as order are beneath him. Things always come up missing. The safe bet is to always go with a plastic bag.

"Be sure to make a bag for your brother," Mom states, sipping her coffee as she tracks my movement with those invisible eyes. In the last five years, I've refined the skill of when to pick my battles. Instinctually, I responded to her request.

"Yes, ma'am."

Still racing against the clock to meet the bus, I quickly pour and zip two bags of Cheerios for me and Eddie. As I finish up, I sling both bookbags over my shoulder and say to Mom in passing,

"Alright Mom, I'm outta' here. Have a great day." She uses her free hand and exerts her motherly strength to stop me in my tracks. As she gets on her feet, she puts down her coffee to give me her undivided attention in the most inopportune moment.

"Hold on, let me look at you." She gives me that motherly scan that results in a smile of approval.

"Alright, lil' momma! With your cute self. You have a great day today." She pulls me in for a quick hug and lets me escape her clutches of love.

Walking towards the front door, I begin to shout upstairs. "Eddie, if you don't hurry up, I'm —"

Gingerly walking down the stairs, he interrupts me and sarcastically says, "I'm going to be lonely without you?"

"That's so nice of you to admit your need for me in your life," Eddie declares with a smirk on his face.

To his comment, I respond in kind. "Nice. very nice." I motion to hand him his bag only to drop it at his feet.

Why am I the one cursed with the baby brother that not only goes to the same school as me but takes the same junior classes? My parents may have blessed him with brains, but knowing him, they forgot to supply him with a healthy dose of common sense.

Eyeing the front door, I turn the knob only to be met with resistance opening towards me. With a big smile, my favorite person in the world walks through the door.

"Hi, Daddy!"

"Hey, baby girl," we say to one another as we hug. Dad, in his peripheral vision, spots my brother trying to become invisible. He quickly snatches Eddie like only a father would and says,

"Get over here boy, show ya' old man some love," removing any chance of him avoiding the group hug action. After a solid ten-seconds, Eddie begins to wrestle out of the hug. "Alright Dad, that's enough. We've got to go to school."

"Well, y'all better get going. I saw your bus down the street. Love y'all."

Eddie and I make our way outside with a purpose.

A couple of paces away from the house, I quickly turn around and shout, "Hey, Dad!" before the door closed.

"Yeah?" he responds.

"Are we gonna' be able to work on the car tonight?"

"For you, I'll make it a top priority, baby girl."

"Okay, thanks; see you later!" I head off to catch the bus waiting for me at the corner.

What a start to a beautiful day.

3

Morning Laps

Like all school buses, our arrival is announced with the tires' high pitch screech bringing us to an abrupt halt in front of the school. The doors fling open and we march single file off the bus like captives coming to grips with their new forced reality that this is home... at least for the next seven hours. After which, we disburse to our accepted social groups for morning social time.

As I walk up the school steps, I put my earphones on my ears. I find that music and headphones are a great deterrent and excuse for not talking and walking past people when you don't want to be bothered. Vanessa at home and Vanessa at school are two different people. I possess this chameleon-like personality where I can turn my charm on and off to adapt to my surroundings. Sometimes I choose to be my carefree self. Other times I decide to blend in and get by. I haven't decided if it's due to the fear of being known, seen, or misunderstood. Growing up in suburbia can do that to you. On the brighter side, this persona gives me ten minutes before the first period to walk the halls and get a spectator's view of the worlds around me.

Living in the suburbs can be a complicated and somewhat defining experience if you pay attention. In the suburbs, some have it all. Their parents have money, and they have access to it, so life is a game of who can be spoiled the most. Then you have the in-betweens; their families meet the minimum requirements to be in the room but are balling on a budget. I find if the family is practical and comfortable with where they are, there is a genuineness to them. However, if you get caught up in the hype and try to run that rat race, just like an illusionist, misdirection becomes their bread and butter. With the mom and dad I have, practicality is the only lens I view life through. You have those who make it in, based on merit, because that's the only thing they can showcase to the public. With my Chillhop music sending me into my creative space, I'm able to immerse myself watching the lives on display.

So much of what kids talk about, how we group ourselves, or what we desire to become is centered around this programmed unknown/known standard. The worth of a person is not really found in a connection. For the most part, yes, Clarrisa and Mike are in love with one another. Still, even in this bubble representation where Henbrooks High is our world, we participate in this unconscious filtration process where we seem to pick, choose, and divide based upon a person's value. Can I live out my fantasies going over to your house? Do you have the money to keep up with what I'm doing this weekend? If you're not on my level, why should we be friends?

I remember in my AP Biology class, Mr. Myers told us when you enter the workforce, always remember it's not what you know. It's who you know.

It made me think about how I would feel about people wanting to know me for their come up? And for what? To have a bunch of money?

But money isn't even real; people are. Shouldn't people say what money is worth, not money dictating what people are worth?

Peeling back another layer, within these separate worlds, there are dividing lines of race. Good ol' race! It always seems to be the thing that precedes and follows the economic dividers. The deeper you explore the worlds and identify the dividers, you begin to realize those dividers are only visible to those who are stopped.

As I come to the close of my lap on the first floor, I march upstairs to gather intel on the second floor. As a black female, I can only speak from what I think, feel, and know. Through my first-hand living and witnessing the black experience, I have surmised that black people exist in these separate worlds. Yet, we all have this common mini-world within us navigating the complicatedness of acceptance, understanding of self, pride, and comfort internally and externally.

Unfortunately, sometimes I feel like even within my race, there's this shared space of unknown tension. I feel like I don't measure up to the high or low standard of being 'Black.' Even that's weird to think... What is *Black*?

What is being *Black?* Are there race indicators like in stats? How do I get my stamp of approval? Do I want a stamp or not want a stamp because *they* say I need a stamp? Did we as a people come up with this, or is it another invisible divider I'm bumping up against? What is White or Asian or Latinx or Indigenous People or any group?

Making my way to my class, I yell at myself, *stop chasing the rabbit!* Which is necessary to rescue myself from the abyss of my thoughts. More times than not, in my wandering mind, I end up with more questions than answers, and that's never comforting.

"Brrring- Brrring- Brrring," repeatedly sounds the school bell.

Only five more periods to go, I think as I head into Mrs. Dotsin's math class.

4

AP English

Sometimes when I'm too through with the day, and I just need to get away, I'll head to my last class of the day during lunch to read and chill. Mr. Davidson is dope. He is one of the few black teachers at this school, and I like how he challenges us. Since we're in AP English, we take on the more difficult readings and assignments, but he has a cool way of assigning homework that makes us think outside of just these four walls. As he would say, "my goal is to equip you to thrive in and out of school and experience life from other perspectives to be a more impactful person." He is also pretty creative, like me. Every month or so, there is a new theme on the door that we have to decode for class participation. Currently posted on the door are five hearts with the following messages on them: M.C. -2015 | F.G. - 2015 | P.C. - 2016 | A.S. - 2016 | "How Many More?"

As I walk into class early and sit at my desk snacking on my leftover Cool Ranch Doritos, I look around the room and think about what type of person you have to be, what type of life you've had to endure, to produce life-changing quotes worth hanging on classroom walls. Quotes from Niche, Gandhi, Newton, Mae Jemison, CS Lewis, Obama, Sojourner, Ramsden, and Malcolm X will give a young person a good head start in life. I think that's why out of all my classes, I like English the most. The subjectivity behind the meaning of the words can annoy most, but not me. I enjoy how I'm able to read something and be invited into a person's mind and utilize their eyes to see, feel, and live Life in a way I may never go through. Life itself can feel small, long, short, crushing, or beyond amazing. I get a warm emotional attachment when I read about people's experiences with Life. It's like for a brief time while reading, I can see how they chose to mold Life or if Life molded them.

Weirdly, I think accumulating all these perspectives gives me a greater advantage of making sense of my own life and gain a grasp on what reality is. Long story short, Mr. Davidison's class is dope.

"What are you reading today, Ms. Whitfield?" Mr. Davidson inquires while entering the classroom.

I quickly chew and swallow my food to respond with, "Just another biography."

Mr. Davidison sitting at his desk peeks out to carry on the conversation. He asks, "Really? Who is this one about?"

"I don't know, some guy named Reginald Lewis. I saw it on my dad's bookshelf and picked it up a little while ago; I've barely started it."

I see Mr. Davidson smirking behind his computer, "Well, if there are any secrets to success, he's one that can provide them."

"So tell me again, how did your dad get you to read so much?" Mr. Davidson asks while sliding out from behind his desk.

Growing a bit of a smirk, I respond, "I don't know. He just reads a lot. My mom does too, so we just kinda grew up with books."

"Well, I am truly impressed with you and your brother. Your dad should teach other parents how to keep their kids involved in reading. There are way too many distractions kids fall prey to nowadays.

I think —"

"Brrring- Brrring- Brrring" goes the lunch bell. The scrummaging sound in the hallway means kids have been released from their short-lived breaks and classes, which is a saving grace. I didn't want to hear another adult share another long-winded story of, "Back in my day..."
Standing up, Mr. Davidson stretches. He walks over to assume his post as the doorman of the class. Mr. Davidson says, "Welp, time to mold the next generation."

November 18, 2016 01:30 PM

"Okay, Class! If I may have your attention, please. With the last ten minutes of class, I want to discuss the remainder of the school year with you."

A hush fell over the English class. Mr. Davidson makes his way from the whiteboard at the front and walks towards the empty desk in the front row to sit down.

"How many of you know what happens at the beginning of November?"

An awkward pause follows behind the suspicious question. Jennifer's lonely hand goes up.

"An election," Jennifer states.

"Yes! Good job. Now I know most of you aren't old enough to vote yet, but you will be in the next year or two. How many are aware that the soon-to-be president is Donald Trump?"

The second awkward pause of the class ensues. Mr. Davidson takes a deep sigh and stands from the desk to take an orator's position to share his thoughts.

"Now, I want to make this clear. This is not a Civics class, and by no means do we discuss politics here. However, because this is AP English, there is a higher requirement for everyone to think critically. And it's my job to push you to meet that expectation."

As Mr. Davidson presents his opening statements, the class grows more nervous about what is to follow in the next five minutes. Mr. Davidson is a bright guy. He knows the only thing on our minds right now is our winter break. I speculate what's going to be said next.

"Assuming most of you don't watch the news, there is a lot of controversy surrounding Trump being selected as America's next president. Mainly, this will be a first for America. We will have a person in the office with a unique background and polarizing persona wielding the power and responsibility of being president. So it got me thinking. Who knows what was the slogan of his campaign?"

With quickness, a section of the room shouted, "**MAKE AMERICA GREAT AGAIN!**" followed by laughing.

Those who didn't join in the collective exclamation joined in a collective eye-roll and audible sigh.

Mr. Davidson let out a small chuckle to himself as these events played out. At this moment, he realized his idea wasn't a good idea. It was a great idea.

"That's correct. Looking at the TV, newspapers, and social media outlets, there is a lot of subjectivity regarding what that means and how people feel about it. So the question remains, what does that statement truly mean? Which brings us to your assignment."

Mr. Davidson makes a B-line for the whiteboard and begins to write and talk at us.

"Your next four creative writings will be centered around the thought of: **Depicting Your Great America**.

The student body let out a symphony of pleading "No's" around the room. So loud that Mr. Davidson has to gesture to corral the room.

"Settle down, settle down! Now, this is a deep assignment. I want you to be able to draw your audience into your depicted America. What is America to you? Has it lived up to being the utopia advertised for you and your family? As Americans, what are the great foundational principles that we should keep? Are there things America and its people should improve on? Showcase a meticulously unique and personal understanding of what America is to you and how it would be for others. From now until the end of the school year, this will be our focus. And your first paper is due when you get back from break."

A symphony of objections became audible in the classroom. Students made their resentment for this assignment felt towards Mr. Davidson. I'm not too happy about this either. I was planning on doing a great deal of nothing this break with a side of comforting entertainment to keep me company.

"Brrring- Brrring- Brrring," the dismissal bell rings to indicate the school day has ended.

This has been a poetic ending to my day of struggle.

5

HOME SWEET HOME

With one smooth motion, I generate the sweet sound of closing and locking the front door. In the background is the fleeting noise of the big yellow bus rolling down the road. I have paid my debt to society, I have clocked out with authority. I am now home free. I veer to the right to place my bookbag on the desk chair in the family room with my elation. The family room is the satellite location where we indirectly rendezvous after a long day. It has the TV, video games, big comfy couches for mid-day naps, the family shared computer, and the infamous wall of books. I rank it the second place to find someone only because it's not where the refrigerator is located.

Once I hang my backpack on the back of the chair, I dig out Dad's book to place it back on the wall. Dad is pretty casual about most stuff, but when it comes to his books, like a library, it must be returned within a reasonable amount of time and in the condition it was found. I found that
out the hard way once.

The wall of books is one of his most prized possessions. It has so many random selections of topics and genres, from 1985 Almanacs to the new age self-help books. He's got "DIY" books for plumbing, George Orwell classics, study bibles, and some scientific theory books. Let's just say, if my dad was selected to go on Jeopardy, he's prepared. Mom lovingly says, "your dad is full of useless facts!" His counter punch to that attack is, "Life's best secrets are kept in books; no harm in learning them."

I place the book back in the Black Biography section, ensuring the bind faces out. I must say it is a pretty impressive wall. When we have guests over, people gravitate towards it. I guess the surprise can lend itself to this unsuspecting guy being an avid reader. After all, my dad is no one special. He's just an HR exec for a contracting company in Northern Virginia. He shared with my brother and me that it was difficult for him to read growing up. He got teased for reading too slow and would always get embarrassed by reading aloud. So growing up, he shied away from reading out of fear. Once he conquered those obstacles and accepted nothing was wrong with him, he wanted us to grow an early love for reading and discovering how we interpret information.

Feeling my stomach growl meant it was about that time for my PB and J snack. As I merrily skip into the kitchen, I pull out the peanut butter and bread from the cabinet. I slide to my right to open up the refrigerator. My search for the strawberry jam is coming up empty. If memory serves me right, I know there was enough leftover from yesterday...

unless...

"EDDIE!!!" I scream with my head in the fridge doing one last scan.

"Eddie! Get down here!" I shout from the kitchen, making sure my voice reverberates in his ears upstairs.

"What!?" he says, making his way down the stairs.

I swear this boy has one speed, *SLOW*.

"Did you eat all the jam?"

"I don't know, shouldn't there be some in the fridge?"

"Yeah, that's what I thought, but there doesn't seem to be any. And guess what? We the only two in the house. So I ask again, did you eat all the jam, big head!?" using a tone mixture of Mom and pissed off sibling.

Eddie cracks a smile from a safe distance on the other side of the island. "I mean, if it was that important, maybe you should have gotten here first."

I slam the refrigerator door because it's in my way of maneuvering around this island. "Ugh! Why'd you do that? You know I always make a PB & J after school."

"So what! Now you can broaden your horizons with something else. I'm doing you a favor," he says while wiping the bread crumbs off his mouth and shirt.

"Oh really? Well, I'm doing you a favor…. you ugly. Deal with it!" I shout in retort while storming around to go into the pantry.

Even though I know there's no strawberry jam in there, I go look to validate my frustration.

"Whatever! You just bein' a Tom Petty because you didn't get a chance to enjoy that sweet sweet-savory jam! Mhm, nothing like it when it just hits your tongue! It's an explosion of joy in ya' mouth."

As he laughs at me, he doesn't realize until the last second I've crept up and taken flight to catch his big head in a headlock.

"Get off me! You messin' up my locks!" He shouts, trying to fight back.

"Should have thought about that before you ate the last of the jam!"

Just as our kitchen royale commences for the title, it's short-lived when the true champions Mom and Dad enter from the backdoor like a surprise WWE plot twist.

"'Nessa! Let ya' brother go!" Mom shouts while carrying a bag of groceries.

"Momma, but he started it!"

"I don't care, now y'all stop that foolishness! Y'all too old for this horse playing in the house." She makes her final statement while placing the bag on the island. Just as she requests, I let him go. Typical Eddie can't resist and has to get the last hit in, getting a cheap shove at me.

"Boy! What did I tell you about hitting ya' sister?" Dad rhetorically asks as he enters. "I don't want to see that again, you hear me!" Dad proclaims with his top dog tone.

"In fact, go outside and bring in the rest of the groceries."

As I watch Eddie make his way out the backdoor, he mumbles all soft, "Man! I can't do anything in this house."

Mom putting the food away says, "Nessa, you gotta' stop picking on your lil' brother. What were y'all arguing about anyway?"

"He ate up all the strawberry jam."

"Here, I saw it was low before I left this morning." She says as she hands me the unopened jar of strawberry jam.

I express my joy with, "Sweet!" and slide over to the counter where the bread and peanut butter are to complete my PB&J mission.

Sitting at the table, Dad summons my attention. "Hey, when you're done with your sandwich, meet me in the garage so we can work on the car. I gotta' go into the office after dinner, so we gotta' put some time in early."

I turned to him while spreading the peanut butter on the piece of bread, "Okay, Daddy."

Internally bummed. That's messing with my nap time.

6

POCKETS OF LOVE

To a fault, my dad is a hoarder of information found in books. To the point where he had the bright idea to restore a car together. We've been working on it for the last two years. Learning about wheel alignments, engine leaks, timing belts, and transmission units. Let's just say it's been a serious process, but I still wouldn't trade it because it's given us time together.

It's formed these pockets of time where my Dad and I can just kick it. We put on some music and just talk, laugh, share, and learn about one another. Sometimes we even learn from one another.

Every girl thinks their Daddy is great. He's the one person nothing can destroy. In these pockets of time, it has allowed him to open up to me and share his concerns, dreams, and wishes for my brother and me. The most precious to me is that he has been able to share his failures. He's shared his story about his suicide attempt in high school when his best friend was killed due to neighborhood violence. He shared his struggles and fears about potentially never getting out of his dead-end hometown. He told me a story about his first job when he moved up to DC from Mississippi. His career was to aid the elderly, mentally and physically challenged people.

For the longest, he hated the job because of the grotesque smells, the grueling hours, and the unprepared situations you're placed in on the daily. The hardest part for him was developing a sense of humility. There he was a 21-year-old, serving people deemed as helpless in the eyes of society for the most part. He had the attitude that he was above this. One day he said I'm tired of being miserable and unhappy, so he made a conscious decision to think, act, and conduct his job with joy and acceptance.

The more he grew in servitude and humility, the more upset he became with himself because his pride kept him from seeing them as people. He described them as people with immense value the world couldn't comprehend. From that job, he met an elderly man that counseled him on how to get into college and steered him on his career path. The most impactful to him was a 21-year-old Peruvian man with a degenerative disease named Javier. Dad says he was the embodiment of all that is great with mankind. Javier's joy to see my dad was everything. It's like he was blessed with the ability to connect immensely with people. Dad said that even when he lost the ability to talk and move, he would spend hours just talking to him, and he could feel Javier's responses and love in his eyes. He said those times were formative years that taught him how to love people, that everyone is worthy of your acknowledgment of their existence, and inherent value can share and teach us something. Dad was everything back when I was younger, but these pockets of time have made him more than everything in my eyes.

"'Ight baby girl, so today we are going to put on these last two new tires and install the new spark plug."

"Cool, Cool," I respond so I can hype myself to lift these tires.

"So roll the first one over here, we're going to start with the driver's side."

"Okay," I reply as I'm rolling.

"So, how was school today?" He asked, sitting on the creeper.

After struggling to roll and lean these massive tires by the car, I take this opportunity to catch my breath. "It was fine. I was just glad to get through it. The only thing that sucks I gotta' do a stupid English assignment over break."

"Oh, really, what's it about?" He asked while holding the lug nuts in his hand.

"We have to like come up with a way to depict what a Great America would look like to us," I say while realizing how out of shape I am.

"Mmmhm, that sounds like an interesting subject matter. Have you thought about what you're going to depict?"

As I take a seat on the cement floor, I say, "Psht, no. The only thing I've been thinking about is what movies and shows I'm going to watch, in what order, and how much sleep I'll need to survive."

He begins to chuckle while looking at me, "Just because you on break don't mean you need to turn off your brain. Trust me, when you become an adult, all these breaks and stuff go away. As you will soon learn, living is expensive."

"Just never be afraid of hard work," he says, in his wisdom dispensing tone. "Alright, now when changing a tire, what tools do you need?"

"A lug wrench and a jack."

"Good, and where are those found in your car?"

With my know-it-all tone, I say, "In the truck underneath the spare tire."

"Nice job. So once you begin the process, be sure your jack is set up properly and stable. Now, once you get the old tire off, you want to set that flat right next to the jack. The reason being, if by mistake while you're changing the tire, you bump the jack, or it slips, the flat tire can serve as a last resort for the car to land on without it landing on you or the floor and potentially not being able to get it up."

I start to nod my head stating, "That's smart. I wouldn't have thought of that."

"Yeah, most people don't know that. Now, when you're changing the tire, you want to get in the squat position like so. And lift." Dad demonstrates.

"Next, you want to use the wrench to screw the nuts back in, in a star- pattern. Again, it's a safe method to get the job done."

After he finishes tightening the last nut in, he hands me the wrench. I take a deep breath and get to work on the last one. Dad's about demonstrating and watching you perform. So I move to the other side and get to work.

"Nice, very nice. Now just do a final check on all the nuts to make sure they are in well." The teacher advises me, the pupil.

"Sweet, you're all done," Dad says while handing me a towel to wipe my hands off.

"Sweet, that definitely ain't easy." I exhaustingly say as I take the towel and wipe the grease... or dirt... or whatever off my hands.

"Never fear hard work, we're built to endure, we're built to accomplish whatever we set our mind to do." My dad is known for sharing quotable statements that seem to be deeper than what the situation calls for, yet I imagine I'll remember them all.

"Hey 'Nessa, you know I was thinking about your project. You should revisit some of those Mcdonald's short books and essays I had you write. You remember those?"

"How could I forget! Torturous! You realize I was like eleven at the time, right?" I said, laughing at the memory of those times. During black history month, we would go to McDonald's weekly to get one of the pamphlets they gave out with each happy meal about the life of significant black figures. The deal was if I got lunch from McDonald's, I would have to prepare a summary paper about what I learned, the significance of that person's work, and how I felt about them. There I was telling my mom on car rides about how Garrett Morgan invented the stoplight or in the summer telling all my friends that a black guy named Lonnie Johnson invented the super soakers we were playing with. Or while in school, I'm presenting my Black History facts on Benjamin Banneker and how his brilliance brought us almanacs, the most accurate woodworking clock, and being a self-educated mathematician and astronomer that finished the design of Washington, DC.

"If I'm not mistaken, those books could still be on the wall. I'm just saying think about the contributions those books taught you that you would've never known about and the contributions these Americans gave us that we still enjoy."

I ponder on his suggestion before I respond. "That's a good point, · I'll mull it —"

The garage door swings open. Here comes Eddie racing down the stairs holding an opened envelope in his hand.

"Dad! Dad! Look at what came in the mail," Eddie says, bursting with joy.

Dad takes the envelope from him and drags out the paper. Our worst nightmare has been realized. Eddie's driver's permit has arrived.

"Oh, Lawd! Be with us," I cry towards the heavens.

"Shut up, 'Nessa!" Eddie retorts.

"Congrats Son, this is great. Look at you becoming a man." Dad says.

"Yes, I am," Eddie responds proudly.

"Hey, Dad. Is it possible we can go driving this weekend? I have to get my hours in with an adult."

Dad ponders what he has going on this weekend. He carefully responds, "If you're committed to doing it early, I can make sure I give you a few hours. I know I have a couple of things I need to do for work, and I gotta' tend to some items for ya' mom and work on ya' sister's car. Let's shoot for like, 8 am Sunday, okay?"

Eddie's excitement is at an all-time high, "Sure, that'll work! Thanks, Dad!" He shouts while heading back up the stairs.

"Alright 'Nessa, why don't you go inside and let me work on the spark plug piece, and I'll show you what I did later; sound good?" Dad bargains.

"Sure! Thanks Dad," I respond.

As I go up the stairs and open the door, I turn around and watch my Dad dig for some tools and dance his way in the depths of my heart and mind.

I used to believe my Dad was everything back when I was younger, but these pockets of time, these moments confirm he's more than everything to my family. Such a blessing, such a blessing.

7

EARLY MORNING HEAVINESS - NOVEMBER 20, 2016

In my heart of hearts, I believe all of us have an obsession with something. Not all obsessions are destructive. It can be to the gym, dedication to hygiene, or serving others. However, those afflicted with the insistent need to start every morning with a pot of coffee can't be trusted.

Dad is one of those people.

I don't know what it is about the aroma, but I can't stand it at all! On the weekends, a little piece of my smell and soul dies because my dad is home in the morning, starting his day with his obsession. He took that stupid jingle, "The best part of wakin' up…" to heart. His joy in the morning turns my stomach, literally. This disdain is not only because of the smell. He likes to carry the scent throughout the entire house super early. So it's not a smell with some distance because it's on the other side of my door, providing a pungent and unwanted wake-up call.

As I begin flailing the covers off me, I read my clock on my desk and ponder, *6:50 am. Well, I might as well get a jump on my laziness for the day. I wonder if there are any Eggos?*

Opening my door, I begin to quietly creep down the stairs, and I'm tickled by the thought of how being one of the first people up early on the weekend is reminiscent of being the first one up on Christmas. Except the only thing waiting for you at the bottom of the stairs is prayerfully a full refrigerator.

Look at my random thoughts getting an early jump on the day. Navigating through the smell, Dad is at the kitchen table with his favorite mug playing jazz softly.

"Mornin' baby girl," He says.

"How'd you sleep?"

"Mornin', mornin'. I slept well Dad, it's what I woke up to that's the disturbing part?" I say to broach the subject about the morning smell.

He responds with, "What you mean?"

I walk over to him, grab his hand ever so kindly and say, "If you could just find it in your heart not to stand outside my door with coffee so I don't have to smell it. I would just be ever so grateful, Father."

I only break out the *Father* when I'm alluding to the fact this sarcasm card is about to be played hard, so brace yourself.

He chuckles as he lovingly snatches his hand back, "Oh sure, sure. I'll make sure to abide by those rules in YOUR house. Last time I checked, this was my house."

As I walk over to the fridge to slide the freezer door open, I respond in kind.

"That's fine. I think I'll make mom aware that you said this is your house 'cus I could have sworn she said this was her house, I must be confused?"

He laughs in his cup, trying to make sure he doesn't spill the coffee on himself. He places it back on the table and concedes. "See now you know that ain't fair. That's called bringing a gun to a knife fight."

"Well hey, I play to win. What can I say?"

I became excited because I found some strawberry Eggos. I pull the box out of the freezer and slide to the left to turn on the oven and pull out a baking sheet from the lower cabinet. As I wait for the oven to warm up, I walk over to the table and pull out a chair.

"What you reading?" I ask, refocusing my attention on Dad.

"Oh, I'm just doing some early morning studying. Mom isn't going to be too happy I'm missing another service, so I thought I'd get a jump and do some studying so I can at least say I read some today without lying."

"Ah yes, yes. You're taking Eddie driving today. Where y'all going?"

"Probably just up to y'all high school. You got the open course right there. So getting it done early will ensure no one else is out there for Eddie to bump into."

As a slightly concerned sister I ask the question, "Are we sure he's ready for this step?"

"Well like it or not he's getting older, and with that, he's going to want the privilege of driving. I just need to make sure he is capable of handling the responsibility."

Looking down, as he rubs his mug softly, he takes a deep breath. He continues with his thought, "It's my duty to make sure he's prepared for all that comes with driving. No matter how difficult it may be for both of us."

I'm a little perplexed by his reply to my surface-level question.

"You okay? Are you nervous about the whiplash you may experience with him?"

As I chuckle, I realize I'm the only one laughing.

"No, I'm not concerned about that. I'm just... I'm praying he's ready to handle the responsibility of driving."

"Beep!" The oven interrupts the flow of our conversation. I walk over and place the baking sheet in the oven. Still confused, I lean against the island and ask, "Hey, can I come along?"

"I don't think that's a good idea, baby girl." My dad says, flipping through his Bible.

"Please Daddy! I wanna watch. I want to see if he's a better driver than me. Plus, I can play the buffer role. You know, keep you two entertained and point out his erroneous steps in a comedic way if I see you starting to get frustrated with him."

"I... I don't know. I mean, he has to focus on what's happening and I'm going to be focused on teaching."

I flip my Eggos to the other side and close the oven. I then turn and respond to his pending denial, "Please Dad, I promise I'll be good. I promise. I promise."

Dad takes a hefty sigh, which is always a good sign for me.

"Okay. I guess it won't be bad for Eddie to learn how to concentrate when he has various passengers in the car. Who knows, it can be a good lesson for you too. You have to promise one thing?"

I nod my head in premature agreement.

"You can't hold anything you see or hear against me. I want you to know everything that may or may not happen is to make Eddie better and a more aware driver."

"Okay cool, cool." I pull out my Eggos, put them on a plate, and turn off the oven. I pour a glass of milk and smother my Eggos in some syrup before I walk off to go into the living room to watch TV.

"Hey 'Nessa, when you're done eating, go wake up your brother, and both of y'all get dressed so we can head out."

"Okay, good to go," I say while walking away.

They say if you pay attention to the signs, you can see the makings of what type of day it's going to be. Perhaps focusing on the smell of the coffee or the joy I have for Eggos distracted me from seeing what's brewing right in front of me.

November 20, 2016 9:15 AM: Henbrooks High Driver's Ed Course

Around and around he goes where he stops, nobody knows!

I standby on the sidelines watching Eddie and Dad circle the parking lot for what feels like the 80th time. I'm stuck sitting on the curb spectating the slowest solo derby race in history. Ah, well, at least I get to catch up on my podcasts & Candy Crush.

"Hey, Big Head! Get in," Eddie shouts at me when he comes to a stop. I pull out my headphones and jump in the back seat.

"So how's it going, Dad?" I ask to inquire about Eddie's progress.

"I'm killin' it! Slowing down properly, coming to complete stops at stop signs, putting my signal on 200 feet while merging over, accounting for blindspots!" Eddie outlines.

With a bewildered look, I say, "Uh... Eddie, it's 100 feet you're supposed to signal..."

"Oh well, hey, I'm a cautious driver. I'll do whatever it takes to get Dad to let me do this on my own." Eddie responds.

Dad, with a stoic look, responds, "So far, so good son. Here, why don't you pull into a parking spot over there to the right?"

Eddie complies with the instruction given. Once he secures the car in between the lines straight, he places the car into park.

"Well, look at you Eddie. I'm impressed," I comment, "You got in straight. Your decision skills are getting better. You didn't choose the parking space with the pole in front of it." Backhanded compliments are a sign of a great brother and sister relationship.

"Nice, Son. Okay, the last thing we are going to practice. I want you to understand how to handle a police interaction. Now—"

"Now Dad, do we have to do this? Eddie interrupts. "I mean, I'm not gettin' pulled over. I'm too awesome for that. And I promise I'm always goin' to do the right thing. Can we practice highway driving instead?"

"Yeah Dad, let's go on the highway! I wanna see Eddie freak out on the highway." I chime in with my recommendation.

"No. We're not going on the highway today. Eddie, pay attention. I need you to pay attention. I'm trying to teach you something vital." Dad implores Eddie.

Eddie expresses his disappointment with a dramatic sigh.

"Now, focus. Whether you are pulled over in the daytime or nighttime; you must be cautious. First, you must use your manners. Yes Sir. No Sir. Yes Ma'am. No Ma'am. Next, ensure that there is clear light in the car's cabin. If it's night time, as you pull over, turn on the lights in the cabin. You need to make sure there's enough light for them to see clearly inside. If you have music playing, turn it off as you are pulling over. Next, keep your hands on the wheel. This is your rest position at all times."

Dad places Eddie's hands through the steering wheel to have them touch the dash.

"Dad, this is weird. Why would I do this? Can't I just keep my hands on the steering wheel?" Eddie asks while moving his hands to a comfortable position for him.

"Eddie, it's not about comfort. It's about compliance. Now, put your hands where I told you." Dad responds.

Eddie slowly returns to Dad's crazy hand position.

"Okay good. Now, when you pull over, the officer will either come to the driver's side window or he may walk from your driver's side back window all the way to your passenger's side front window. Either way, be attentive. Be alert. They will knock on the window. Show them your left hand and slowly press the button to let down the window. After this, you return your hand back to the rest position. You follow me so far?"

"Yeah," Eddie responds. I'm kind of just sitting back here trying to understand why these instructions are so long and taking forever. It's not that hard.

"Now, when he or she asks you for your license and registration, before you move, you verbalize to them where it is and ask if it is okay to reach for it. You do not move until they say yes. Once they give you the go-ahead, you show them your right hand, and you slowly move to grab the documentation. Once you have it, show it in the air, and then slowly move towards them to hand it over."

"Dad, why I gotta' do all these slow movements? It makes no sense. They just asked me for some stuff why I gotta' do all this extraness in between."

Dad makes a heavy sigh and responds, "Eddie, do you want to learn the responsibility it takes for you to drive? If not, we can go home. I'm cool with whichever. You let me know?"

Eddie retreats with his statements, "Okay, okay. No, I want to stay."

"Okay then. If we're going to stay, then you must learn this. This is a part of the responsibility. You're going to have to prove to me you're capable of handling this situation."

"Now, as I was saying, get back into the rest position. At this point, he or she may walk away or may ask you a few questions. Some will be rhetorical and some may be real questions. Answer every question directly and honestly. Before they walk away, you can ask them why you are being stopped."

"Son, now a few other things. You and 'Nessa are quick with your words. If and when you get pulled over. Both of you, this is not a time for games and not a time for jokes. You will not do that during these times. These moments require your attention, your resolve, and, most importantly, you must be in charge of your emotions. The name of the game is: **Get home safe. Get home alive.**"

"Okay Dad," Eddie says, feeling like this lesson is longer than the semester of driver's Ed.

"Repeat the last thing I said." Dad requires.

"Get home safe. Get home alive." Eddie parrots back.

"Good, good," Dad says. Evidently, this speech is weirdly weighing on him given his body language.

"So... freeway bound?" I blurt out to cut this unnecessary tension in the air. I mean, I get it, cops have guns, but there are more good cops than bad. At least the math supports Eddie getting home. I conclude, Dad is paranoid. I mean, we live in Leesburg, Virginia. Like, one of the better suburbs of Northern Virginia. It's nothing like stories you hear about in urban areas.

"No, I told you we aren't doing that today, 'Nessa. Just pay attention. In fact, we're going to practice this interaction. 'Nessa, I want you to get up here in the front seat. Eddie, this is what I want you to do: drive the car about a block or so up the road then come back in the parking lot.

35

I'm going to pretend to be a police officer and pull you over. Then we're going to act this out."

"Ooo, an acting job!" I shout as I get out of the back seat. "Should I play the role of the sassy black female or perhaps the aloof passenger unaware of all that's happening around her?"

I quickly crack the door. "I expect compensation to come in the form of pizza. You know, for my time and skills."

"Lil' girl, shut the door," Dad says to me before walking over to Eddie's side.

I think to myself, *why is he being so extra about this stuff? Goodness, I'm just trying to be funny. He said we were quick with it... Do I know how to shut it off? Do I want to shut it off is the bigger question?*

Dad gestures thumbs up to Eddie and Eddie gives one back to him before firing up the car. As we pull away from Dad, there's this photographic moment in my head of watching Dad rubbing his hands together, pacing back and forth in the side mirror. Perhaps he's getting into character.

"How you feelin' bro?" I ask Eddie while he makes this left at the green light to get onto the main road.

"Cool cool, why is Dad being so extra? I don't get it. I understand cops are the authority figures on the road. You should... are supposed to respect that authority. I get how to do that, I mean, we are black." Eddie says, venting.

"Well hey, he's just trying to get you to understand and prove to him you can do it. Fix ya' face, it's still a great day. Just pass this test and we'll probably get some food after." I chant to Eddie to get his head back in the game.

"Yeah you right, you right! I just gotta' get through this."

As we come to a stop at a red light, Eddie turns on the left signal light. He asks," How do you think driving with Mom would be?"

I snicker and respond, "She's a hoot. First off, she doesn't like driving at all, so I feel like she would be on edge the entire time. Which would produce some hilarious moments to talk about over family dinner."

As Eddie makes a U-turn, we share a laugh and head back down. We drive two blocks down to make a right turn and pull back into the school lot. We make the first left and Dad steps out in front of the car with his hand out indicating he wants Eddie to stop.

"Here we go. Police Officer Dad." Eddie says aloud. We laugh as he places the car in park. Eddie's hands drop to the bottom of the steering wheel.

Dad walks over to Eddie's side of the car and taps on the window. I see Eddie raise his left arm to let down the window. After this, he places his hands back on the bottom of the steering wheel.

"License and registration," says Dad, in his commanding voice.

8

GOOD COP. BAD COP.

"Yes, Sir. My wallet and registration are inside the console. May I grab it?" Eddie asks Officer Dad.

"Go ahead and get it." He responds attentively.

Eddie swings around and begins to dig in the center console. While he's digging around in there, he tries to spark a conversation. "How's your day going, Officer? Wonderful, I hope,"

His remarks are met with silence. Eddie's comments died to the erratic rummaging of him looking for his paperwork.

"Young man, I just need to see your papers."

Eddie turns back towards the window and sits still for a quick moment to think about where he placed his license.

"Oh, yeah!" Eddie exclaims as he digs in his back pocket to retrieve and hands his license to Officer Dad.

Dad slowly takes his ID and responds with, "Thank you. Were you able to find your registration?"

Dad is steadily taking mental notes of all of Eddie's mistakes. From being fidgety to not returning to the rest position, he is clearly unprepared for this test. I slide over more towards the passenger door to view this train wreck of an incident better.

"Is this your car?" Officer Dad asks.

"Yes... No! It's a family car. My parents own it." Eddie stumbles onto a final answer.

"Okay. Now, do you think they placed it in the glove compartment?"

"Possibly. Do you want me to check?" Eddie inquires.

With a massive sigh, Officer Dad places his hands on his waist, "Yes. I would like you to check the glove compartment."

"Okay, cool," Eddie says before he unbuckles his seat belt and reaches on my side to open the glove compartment. Eddie is digging around, agitatedly throwing papers in my lap. I glance over and facetiously smile and wave at Dad, commending him for his commitment to his role. He just looks off in exhaustion.

"Sir, I'm not sure what a registration form looks like. Could you —"

"Okay. Cut, cut." Dad proclaims.

"Okay son, you did practically everything wrong. What are you doing? You're not focused! Do you remember any of my instructions?" Dad says in a louder tone.

"Yes, Dad," Eddie says.

"Clearly, you don't. First off, why are you moving around so much? Second, where are your hands supposed to go?"

"Through the wheel on the dash," Eddie's answers.

"Okay, then why did I only see you do that one time? Also, you kept moving and darting with no notification as to what you are doing. You also turned your back to me when you went into the center console and the glove compartment. Never turn your back. Always, always notify the Officer what you are about to do."

As Dad runs through the detailed version of why Eddie failed this part of the driving test, I can tell Eddie is getting frustrated. He doesn't like getting called to the carpet, primarily since it rarely happens. So I can see that none of this information is sinking in by the way he keeps exaggerating his gripping motion back and forth on the steering wheel.

"Now, look in the glove compartment. I had it all neat, but you went and jacked it all up. Do you know what the registration for the car looks like?" Dad inquires as he takes a break from scolding Eddie.

"Yes, Dad! I do—" Eddie says.

"Now, why you lyin'? If you do, then why didn't you grab it? Son, if you don't know just say you don't know. I rather teach you now than you learn this on the fly with an actual cop. Now, I keep all the registrations sticking out of the manual, which is on top so you can grab it with one hand."

"Yeah," Eddie says in a tone you can barely hear. Something tells me I should jump in here before this situation gets out of hand.

"Eddie, what's your problem?" Dad says in a stern voice.

Losing his temper briefly Eddie responds, "I know Dad! I know how to drive and I know how to talk to someone. You just make me nervous, alright!? Like come on, is all this even necessary?"

"Okay, guys, how about we just take a break? Possibly call it a day, get some ice cream to get back to that good ole lazy Sunday." I say, trying to interrupt the foreseen collision of this conversation.

Dad's eyes shoot a look and I know my saving grace would be to mind my business and mouth. I just turn back around and sit quietly. Dad turns back to Eddie.

"Son, I'm not trying to embarrass you. I'm trying to teach you something. You want to drive the cars I own, you must know how to do this. I don't need you to guess, and I don't need you to make excuses why you aren't doing the right thing. You understand me?"

Scolded Eddie responds, "Yes Sir." He can't audibly say what's on his mind because he would die. He gestures to look at his clock as if he has better things to do. Unfortunately for Eddie, Dad saw that. I saw that. God saw that.

Dad concludes this exchange by saying, "You don't believe me? You don't see I'm trying to help you. Okay, go out and circle back. We're going to run it again from the top."

"Yes Sir," Eddie sarcastically says.

Dad steps to the side, after which Eddie pulls off and circles around to head for the light. As we sit at the red light waiting for the traffic light, the silence is paper cutting me to death.

"So.... you mad?" I say to sever the silence.

"Oh, my God! What do you think?! This is so stupid!" Eddie responds.

The traffic light clearly wanted Eddie gone judging how fast the light switched to green. As we make our way down the street, Eddie decides to pour out his emotions.

"Am I wrong? Like bro, what did I do? I'm still a new driver! This is ridiculous how bad he's riding me on this. Okay sheesh! Get off my back about this whole thing. I'll learn, I'll get it together eventually."

"I mean, you were nervous. You know it kinda reminds me of that time when you tried to pick up that girl in the mall, you remember?" I say smiling through my teeth.

Eddie lets out a chuckle he was trying to hold in. "Whatever Vanessa, you're not funny."

I grab myself as if a chill went up to my spine, "Ugh! Now, my good Sir, you didn't have to go there. That's personal!"

"Whatever. I'm just saying Dad's acting as if we live in Woodbridge or Dale City or PG County."

As Eddie makes this U-turn to head back to the school, I try to help diffuse the situation.

"Dad's just being Dad. Learn, or at least fake it so we can get through this situation."

"Whatever, I don't even care anymore. I can't even remember the things he was yelling about." Eddie says.

"Well, you better start remembering, we're right here," I respond quickly as we make the right turn to enter the school.

"Whatever. Dad wants to treat me like a bad kid. I'mma act like a bad kid." Eddie says, readjusting himself in his seat.

As Eddie makes the next left turn, a slight shiver goes up my spine. Family disputes are like a train wreck. You watch the disaster with some clear distance.

Officer Dad holds out his hand for Eddie to slow down. Eddie fires the first shot by stopping further than Dad to make him walk a couple of paces to the car. Dad walks up slowly and knocks on the window.

"Hey, um... why didn't you stop where I told you to?" Officer Dad utters.

"Oh, sorry about that. My brakes are a little worn. Anyways, is there a problem?" Eddie askes while one hand is on the steering wheel and one in his lap.

"First. I'll be asking the questions. Second, please place your hands on the steering wheel so I can see them at all times."

Eddie sighs and flagrantly places his other hand on the steering wheel. I begin to let off a little anxiety by rubbing my seatbelt.

"License and registration, please."

Eddie responds with, "Sure thing, Officer." Eddie reaches over without hesitation for the glove compartment and with matching, quickness Officer Dad screams out,

"Hey! What are you doing!? Put your hands back where I can see them!"

Eddie is surprised. Not at being yelled at, but the way he was yelled at. It was a different type of aggression in his tone neither of us had heard before. The words slammed Eddie back into his seat.

"Yes, Sir. I just have to reach in the glove compartment to get the registration. Is that okay?"

"Are there any weapons or illegal items in your glove compartment?"

"No, Sir." Seems like Eddie has abandoned whatever idea he had about being bad. I guess giving out disrespect didn't command the respect he wanted. Perhaps the new approach will help.

Officer Dad provides him with the following orders, "Alright. Go ahead. Slowly!"

Eddie slowly reaches for the glove compartment with one hand while keeping the other on the steering wheel. He eyes and retrieves the envelope sticking out of the manual and closes the compartment back. As he returns to the resting position, he slowly passes it to Officer Dad. As Officer Dad is reviewing the registration, he speaks at Eddie,

"So I guess you want to go to jail for driving without a license, right?"

"No, Sir. I have my license."

"Then why isn't it in my hands?"

Eddie responds with, "I apologize. Let me give it to you." As he offers his apologies to gain retribution for his missteps, he inadvertently commits new missteps. Nervously, he scrambles in the driver's side door panel with no luck. He then begins to self-frisk his front pockets for his ID with no luck. Returning to the resting position, I can tell Eddie is drawing a blank and is not thinking well on his feet. So I offer him some guidance.

"Eddie, ask to check the middle."

"Oh yeah!" Eddie exclaims. However, those weren't supposed to be the only words that came out of his mouth. He turns his back again towards Officer Dad and this transgression seems too unforgivable.

"Hey! Out of the car! Out of the car right now!" Officer Dad says while taking a step back.

Eddie and I look at one another. We are supremely lost in what's happening right now and our frozen posture shows that. Eddie thinks of something to say.

"Is... Is that necessary, Sir? I think my ID is in my center console. I was just trying —"

Marching towards the door and whipping it open, Officer Dad exclaims, "I said, get out of the car now!"

Dad persists in pulling on Eddie's arm as if he is velcroed to the seat and applying a little pressure to the pull will get him out of the car. He forgets Eddie is strapped into the seat, so the quick game of tug-of-war for Eddie's body between the seatbelt and Officer Dad begins.

"Hey, wait! My seatbelt, Sir, my seatbelt." Eddie cries out.

"Wait! Dad hold up! Dad, stop!" I add to Eddie's cries. Yet our sincere pleas for his attention and resolve fall on deaf ears. The fight for Eddie being in or out of the car continues for a few pulls until Eddie has the good sense to undo his seatbelt so he can get out of the vehicle with the next pull. However, Eddie doesn't have the good sense to stop his instincts from fighting for control of his arm. As Eddie stumbles out of the car, Officer Dad shoves him to the ground and locks Eddie's hands behind his back. As he begins to pick himself and Eddie off the ground, he slams the driver's door and Eddie, in that order. My mind is all over the place because I thought this was supposed to be a simple Sunday driving lesson. Against my better judgment, I get out of the car, hoping my calm heart can get this scene back on script to a calmer dialogue.

I open my door and peek my head up. I see Dad pressing his shoulder into Eddie while holding his hands behind his back.

"Dad! DAD! Calm down! I think Eddie —" I shout.

Officer Dad shouts back, "Get back in the car! I didn't tell you to get out!"

"Dad!"

Officer Dad adds his finger into the mix to further convey his point, "I said get back in the car!"

My mind and my heart are thoroughly confused because I'm seeing my father act like someone I don't know. My head is telling me to do what's in the best interest of myself. *Get in the car.*

My heart is pushing me to stay out of the car and help my little brother. That's what you do when you care for someone in trouble. You do something. As I open my door as if to get back in, I don't get in. I stand there watching my father tussle with my brother for position, leverage, and control. No longer is the situation about a routine stop. This situation has morphed. This situation is being fed by this self-preservation on one side and evoking of position from the other. There's no strategic execution for a mutually desired outcome. The outcome has changed to who's going to have the edge. Who will not be denied, the authoritative figure or the 'unwilling to comply with the rules', individual. Clearly, both feel they are in the right to impose on the other.

"Now! I told you to get out of the car! Why didn't you do so? When I tell you to do something, you are to comply! Do you understand?!"

He shouts at Eddie with his shoulder pressing into Eddie to control him.

"I pulled you out of the car because I didn't see or know what you were reaching for. I could no longer see your hands. I gave you a pass the first time, and yet you continued to move excessively without any notice. What were you doing?"

"Sir, I was just trying to grab my ID. I think my wallet is in the center console."

"Well, maybe you should have thought about saying that before you moved!"

"Stop moving! Do you hear me?!" Officer Dad shouts.

"Maybe if you stop pressing into my back! This hurts, Dad! Okay, Dad, stop. I don't want to do this anymore."

As they continue to tussle, Officer Dad explains, "It's not supposed to feel good. Now you've been giving me an attitude this whole time. When I say something, I expect you to comply fully, you hear me?!"

Eddie shuffles around to try and find a restful position between Officer Dad's shoulder and the car.

"Look, Dad! Stop, you're hurting me!" Eddie exclaims, still unwilling to stop struggling.

Eddie's not fighting for control. He's fighting to get out of this painful situation; why can't Dad see that?

"Look, I'm ordering you to stop resisting! Do you hear me!?" Officer Dad proclaims.

Eddie summons all his strength into his right arm, and with one motion, he frees his right arm and spins towards Dad. Maybe he figures if Dad sees his tears, it'll snap him out of character. Once Eddie turns face-to-face with his assailant, the scene comes to a haunting, frightening end with one last exclamation and gesture.

"BANG!" Officer Dad screams out with his fingers in the position of a gun pointed against Eddie's head.

Officer Dad, Eddie, and I don't move. The only thing moving are tears racing down our faces.

Sunday driving lesson: **Get home safe. Get home alive.**

9

Deep Dive into Reflection

The mind is a fascinating unknown. Scientists say there are two types of minds: The conscious mind and the unconscious mind.

Both play a massive role in one's existence, yet the unconscious mind seems to be the most susceptible to deceit.

It's crazy when you realize your brain and mind are always on, operating, firing, downloading information, giving out commands, and being programmed. Some things you're aware of since it's based upon what you see, hear, touch, or experience. Yet, there are images, implicit messages, words that are said, actions done all around you that your mind captures unknowingly, yet it affects you. Over time slight changes create behaviors and thoughts that mold you to its will.

Today started so calmly, and yet it went *wayyy* left. Maybe my unconscious mind was seeing the bread crumbs and sending a signal my brain couldn't decode.

After a day like today, I find myself camped out in the living room in the reflective position upside down on the couch, looking at the bookshelf to make sense of everything. This was one of those moments where my conscious and unconscious mind couldn't join forces to embrace the magnitude of the moment.

It's like my mind has this enormous pile of laundry inside. Despite the basket being in the middle of the room. Despite the uncontrollable pile spilling over and on the verge of toppling, the easiest thing to do is... walk around it. Ignore it out of pure terror because the level of effort that must go into conquering this mountain is too much.

I hear the clock on the desk tick for every passing second. Accompanying the clock is the fleeting parts of my parents' conversation in the kitchen.

"James, I can't believe you did that?!" Mom says.

"Baby, he wasn't listening. You weren't there. What was I supposed to do?"

"Anything other than pointing your finger at him like a gun. I don't want him terrified."

TICK. TOCK.
TICK. TOCK.

"I need him to be prepared. Do you think I wanted to do this?!"

"I couldn't sleep last night. How do you tell your kid you must follow some unwritten rules unless your very life is in jeopardy?"

"Don't you think this is important?" Dad says.

"Of course, it's important. I see the crazy killings happening too," Mom says.

TICK. TOCK.

"Baby, we can't protect them forever, especially him. No matter how hard we try. Just because we're out here in the suburbs doesn't mean it can't happen to him."

"All I'm saying is I wish you could have just found a different way or not have been so caught up in the moment yourself. He may be scarred for life. Do you realize that? Vanessa too."

TICK. TOCK.
TICK. TOCK.

"James, I know it's not an easy job to teach him how to be a black man because it's difficult teaching her to be a black woman. I just don't want them to fear what people might think of their blackness then immediately think the worst of what people might do because they are black."

TICK. TOCK.

"Neither do I, but I do not want them to be oblivious to the fact that some people won't be comfortable with them being black. And sometimes those people carry guns."

TICK. TOCK.

"I'm sorry, I'll talk with Eddie. I admit I did take it a little overboard. I'll fix it. Is that his plate wrapped up over there?"

TICK. TOCK.

The sound of footsteps coming closer and closer broke me out of my daze enough to sit up. Dad was standing there with a foil-wrapped plate of food and Eddie's favorite drink. He and I lock eyes, and we share a burdened smile.

"Hey, baby girl... I'm sorry about today." Dad humbly says to me.

"Don't worry 'bout it," I say, accepting his apology.

He nods his head and goes upstairs to Eddie's room.

A father's job is never done.

I get back to my upside-down view of the bookshelf. Thinking... just thinking...

TICK. TOCK. TICK. TOCK. TICK. TOCK.

The simplicity of a clock is so elegant. There's no debating, no feelings, no power struggle. There's just a purpose. The clock either performs the task correctly or incorrectly. If it's incorrect, then you take the necessary steps to make it perform right. Benjamin Banneker probably figured that out way before me. Too bad humans are way more complicated and depending on where you are and how you are programmed, your brokenness could be by design.

Staring at the wall of books, I'm hit with the idea that perhaps this wall means so much to Dad because it's more than just a collection of books. This wall is a collection of accomplishments. It's a wall of pain, endurance, hurt, struggle, confusion, turmoil, purpose, collective and individualistic success. Whenever I read something extraordinary about another black person's achievements from the past, all it does is make me proud to bear the color I've been blessed with. From Garrett Morgan, Benjamin Banneker, to Toussaint L'Ouverture. I still remember the fascination I had at twelve spending the summer with Dad tracing the origins of the phrase "Give Me The Real McCoy" from the brilliant mind of Elijah McCoy. Or how the warm comfort of inspiration would whisk me off to sleep as I thought about the milestones of black women Mom read to me as bedtime stories. I even grew an appreciation for ironing my clothes when I learned Sarah Boone's ingenuity brought it to existence.

Lying with tears racing down my face, I realize I'm a spectator to my mind's sponsored race through the thoughts, unanswered questions, and hard revelations of reality. I quickly turn over to sit up on the couch to embrace a solo therapy session.

I'm frustrated.

I'm upset.

I'm confused... I'm torn.

I feel like someone is trying to rip something precious from my grasp. I'm doing everything I can to get a grip on this inescapable situation, but it seems like I'm failing with every passing moment.

What am I to do about racism? What is racism? What qualifies a person as a racist? Which is more critical, the spoken words or the actions shown? What's a true reflection of what is in your heart? How can you ever honestly tell?

People lie all the time!

People say one thing but do another every day, regardless of color. Is someone saying, I don't like black people, worse than someone else committing violent acts that harm only black people? Are both enough to qualify them as racist? Or is one simply more racist than another? Is it weird that I think their honesty of knowing they don't like me for being black provides me an inside track on how to overcome them because I know where they stand?

Am I conditioned to think that when someone does something and has a particular skin color, it's a justifiable leap to conclude maybe they have some deep racist seeds within them? When a white person and a black person say the same word, why am I liable to give a white person the side-eye? Why do I go into detective mode and say, "now out of all the words you could have chosen, you chose that one. Why?" *Does that make me racist?*

It's true "thugs" is a factual term used to describe someone who has chosen to act and live a life that potentially harms others. They can be a person seeming to be at odds with the law. But isn't it interesting when a white male or a group of white men do something, the consensus is to label and treat them as "troublemakers" because the rule has shown and taught that bad white kids equal isolated incidents. That they will grow out of this behavior that's beneath them and shouldn't caste a prejudice assumption. But blacks and browns are typically referred to as thugs because they are the standard to this term.

We have all learned to make the following association: blacks & browns equal thugs until key identifiers clue you in that they are an exception to such rigid standards, but still reserve those semi- drawn defensives because the negative representations and perceptions supersede the good. At some point, they will revert to their true self.

Surely that must be so. Who gave people the authority to caste that judgment? Teach us all this way of mislabeling? Or is it really mislabeling, depending on the labeler. Don't forget blacks and browns aren't given distinction by age or gender. It's a collective assumption that doesn't see those factors.

Nevertheless, *is it crazy that I agree?*

I agree it's wrong to blame a person for using the same language I know a black person would use, but if they're white, I assume it's racist. Couldn't the black person be just as programmed to see his own as they want you to and describe your own like that, but if a black says it, it's okay. Similar to good hair versus bad hair. Whites seem to just KNOW they have good hair, but us blacks continue the debate and qualify our hair amongst ourselves which reinforces their security and our insecurity.

Am I conditioned to come to that realization?

How can I determine if a racist person is in pursuit of my demise? Should I care if you're racist only... or should I only care if you are a racist that is driving some purposeful action?

I don't like short guys. Does that make me a heightist? No, I'd like to think that's my preference and I don't treat short guys with disdain when they are around me or come up to me. I could become a heightist if I decide to run for office and back bills and push narratives that sterilizing all men below 6ft is a good thing and needed because they don't deserve to cultivate children or studies show short men are more violent. Therefore, they deserve society to back or shoulder the responsibility to aid in levying a noble harshness upon them due to their biological aggression. They are doing a disservice by populating more of my non-preference. Or worse, lessening the amount of men above six feet by cross-procreation, but I hide it behind theories and other emotional driven terms people can focus on besides my actual intent.

What do you do when the rhetoric someone spews is wisely chosen to not publicly showcase their stance, yet you are quoted by those that feel emboldened to make their worldview of blacks known? Isn't it a logical assumption to think you're at least comfortable with the open hostility towards minorities? And perhaps your double message pleases the group to know that they have a spy in the ranks?

If I'm not mistaken, the court of law will consider me an accessory to a crime despite my cries of not being directly involved. I am subjected to being deemed just as guilty, and it is up for debate if I had an opportunity and responsibility to do the right thing and failed to do so.

The court of law and the court of the people seem to be at odds. If done correctly, you can play both sides. We've seen many accomplish that.

Have I allowed myself to be conditioned?!

Is this all just too complex of an issue to boil down to one thing? Or how do I move in a way that's righteous enough to know how to adequately divide right and wrong but humble enough to make it attractive for all to want to emulate?

Why do white people operate the way they do?

Why do they say phrases like "I don't see color." Although, when they are in a situation when they don't have warranted control, they magically claim their whiteness and identify your blackness through action and solicit expedited police-type help to regain control.

"I don't feel safe! Help, please. I feel threatened!" Are some go-to phrases white people scream in a threatening tone to convey their whiteness and your perceived threatening skin color which is synonymous with aggression but, you have black friends.

Is it all the way fair for me to cast pre-judgment on whites because of the sins of their lineage of American people? The whites here and now didn't originate these problems; they just seem to be the ones being paid the dividends of the investments of the past, knowingly or unknowingly. Send anyone a free check, they're going to claim it no questions asked. Is it possible, just as we are all conditioned to view blacks and browns as lesser and more dangerous, we are programmed to think of whites as the other way?

What do we, as black people, want?!

It's not like we are the most united! Look at the difference between football and basketball players. In one sport, players are united for a cause; they receive protected pay. Past owners' sins aren't being bestowed on today's owners, just the accountability to do better when better is required. Football seems to have an American history stance on the relationship between players and owners. Even college players suffer under that same mindset. I wonder what the color ratios are?

Why can't we as blacks be united? Why are we so strained? Despite being aware of our strain of division, we still choose to operate in that division. I wonder what it would be like if the atrocities experienced in America occurred overseas, and when liberated, we sought refuge in America. Some argue that we, as blacks, are our own worst enemy and that the math doesn't support the popular narrative of the black struggle.

Whites are 25% more likely to die at the hands of police officers, is a stat I've read before to argue that blacks' plight is fictitious and that being killed by a cop is less likely for someone like my brother. Somehow the confinement and protection of these numbers don't provide me the comfort they say it should. History around me doesn't suggest that if that's the case why aren't whites protesting that they are dying at an alarming rate by police? Should we just accept the risk because, at the end of the day, we are all only numbers, right? That doesn't sit well in my heart.

Is it possible to operate in a racist manner unconsciously because you are unconsciously aware of your societal superiority? I mean, if you are blissful in your ignorance maybe you're not trying to hear about anyone's plight because it bothers your comfort. I know how frustrating it is when someone wakes me up out of some good sleep...

If laws have removed the ability to inflict racist acts and behaviors towards people, why would the average white person not want to trade lives with a black person if all is equal? Is racism just the exposed part of this glacier we call America? How do we operate around this glacier? Casteism?

Am I crazy to think differences are points of uniqueness and importance in each other... not points of contention and comparison?

That's why I've never said I don't see color. In fact, I acknowledge all color because it is a part of you that at the minimum, should be respected and part of what you bring to the table. We all should be comfortable recognizing and championing something so sacred. At the very least, we should be able to be nice, but sometimes that comes off unreasonable. When I think of the founding fathers' words, the goal at the minimum was to be able to think, believe, and be you without physical harm. At that point, it's incumbent upon me not to read more into it or make a situation because I may or may not know what you think of me.

At the same time, am I ready for a white person to recognize my blackness and see me beyond the negative? If this happens, it will force me to assume the responsibility of seeing them as white and not racist.

What makes up the societal heart?

We are taught that laws point us towards a moral utopia and balanced fairness and justice. Could laws have inserted thoughts, feelings, and emotions inside both groups of people and have done terrible harm to both sides?

It's hard to admit.... many laws that were once thought of as good, have been removed. Sadly, I think it was done far too late in that the seeds were planted and harvested time and time again. One thing the government can't do is legislate feelings and how we choose to treat people.

Maybe that's our core grievance? Fix your heart!

The fact that the Negro Code was a real thing speaks to the craziness of the time; to outline the law on the type of fabric and color a black could wear is scary detailed. Too detailed to NOT say that it was put in place for a particular lasting outcome. As my uncle would say, you can move smart or be enslaved to your emotions. Sometimes I feel like we choose the latter because at least we are the master and the slave. The problem is we aren't fully free.

The levels to this thing are deep!

There are so many twists and turns that can leave you drowning in the deep end of thoughts to a point where you just want out instead of searching for the solution. Four hundred plus years of actions, systems, implicitness, evil, caste-based rhetoric has been spewed out to where it blurs everyone's vision. It's interesting, in Jesus' day, it was ethnicity and tribalism that drove division and it has evolved into a race, color, and tribalism issue. I remember Mom saying how in all this senselessness, we ask where God is, but we forget that we are His image-bearers and the answer is found in the collective Us. Yet the collective Us is being rejected for the selected Few.

People are so complicated. How we think, feel, and move is beyond my level of understanding. How can blacks get genuine compassion to take place? I'm talking about the two-part compassion system.

America's minds are shown disturbing, harsh images and stories of animals being harmed. Then the call to action followed is meant to have a collective positive change. Despite the numbers and statistics, it shouldn't sit well that a family could be on the wrong side of that statistic and should just chalk it up to bad luck or his or her actions warranted the ultimate result of death.

It's interesting we've been in search of this utopian state throughout the history of humanity. At least what movies and books have taught me, the problem in creating a utopian place, it must be built upon the backs of others accepting their misfortune and suffrage.

Is life about power?

Who has more power than America?

This is crazy! I shout as I jump up to put a halt to my mind and tears.

Pull it together 'Nessa. This is just how America is.

Pacing in the room, I do two laps and count to ten around the couch. As I come to the desk, I fixate on Eddie's History book. After a few moments standing there a shock wave travels through my mind to clear all thoughts except one. I pull out the chair and bring up a Word document.

As I begin to type, my singular thought connects to another and another and another.

I say to myself, "This will be my America."

<u>SECTION 2</u>

10

Woke Up Black - Fri. May 6, 1831

The moon lookin' real still and bright tonight!

I say to myself sittin' out in front of the shack house. Almos' like it's lookin' fo' an eye full of some of the torture the Sun saw today. Harsh days is all we see; all we know.

Ain' nothin' else to do, 'cept to just go on and accept it. Wait on the Lor-

Wait on....

Nobody.

As I keep lookin' up, I shake my head fightin' the thoughts that 'dis hear it. Sufferin' through pickin's, beaten's, and hate. May get time wit' my family here and there, but who's to say, I'll be here wit' my family always? I don't own my family to have a say.

"Reagor, boy. You bes' get inside and get ya' rest. We gotta' be in that cane field come sunrise. Boy, you hear me?" Momma say, standin' in the doorway.

"Yes, Ma'am. You gon' to bed. I'll be in, in a 'lil while." I reply, sittin' on the edge of the porch lettin' my feet dangle. Sometimes the swingin' of my legs give my feet the rest they need to work another hard day.

"Okay, baby. Well, be sho' to see Johnny come in. He down there at Mary's shack. Once he gets in, both of y'all come in and get some rest."

"Yes, Ma'am."

What Momma don't know is, I don't sleep at night. I can't let that trouble come in here again.

Sleepin' in 'dis here old wooden shack wit' these floors ain't no easy rest noway. One bed for four people don't work no way. As the oldest, it's my job to make sho' Momma, Sam, and Johnny-Boy get the lil' comforts we allowed. I make due wit' the chair, fireplace, and the extra shirt I got last year.

Massa' Mills said I did well 'nuff job to earn a second shirt fo' the winter.

As the night breeze caresses my blisterin' feet, I see my brother come walkin' up in the distance. As happy as can be, holdin' somethin' to his mouth. As he gets closer, I can see he's happy since he got him somethin' to eat.

"Hey Johnny- Boy, where you get that bread from?" I ask him.

"Mary's momma gave me a piece of bread. It was fo' helpin' Charlie wit' the lumber cuttin'. Why you sittin' out here? I saw the Overseers drankin' by the big house. They maybe comin' round this evening." Johnny-Boy says while steppin' up on the porch to walk on past me.

"'Dat's why I'm sittin' right here."

As I look ova' my shoulder, I say, "Hey Johnny, can I have a piece?"

"Where ya' bread at?" Johnny asks, needin' a decent reason to share.

"I gave my piece to Momma 'dis mornin'. She was shakin' again."

"Oh... okay here." Johnny says while he rewards me what's left of the bread. I turn to gladly receive and salvage every bite.

"I'mma gon' turn in. 'Night Reagor." Johnny says to me as he goes inside.

"Night." I offer up in response.

As I finish my bread, I hobble down slowly to the ground, careful not to hurt my feet. I shuffle up to the hill just behind our shack house off to the right. As I walk, I begin to practice countin'.

"One...Two... Three... Four... Five... Six... Seven... Eight... Nine...Ten... Eleven," I say to myself.

When I can, I like to come here and stand on 'dis little hill. Daddy used to say, "the way the moonlight shines on ya' it look like God's attention is on ya". 'Dis hill was our place. I 'member when he took me here and put me on top 'dis hill here, and I would just feel loved.

As chil'ren ya' get to run, jump, laugh, and imagine. 'Den as ya' get bigger and get called to go to work you realize. I ain't a child no mo', just another nigger slave. Only decision as a slave you get is rather you gon' feel what comes ya' way or not. If you don't know, Massa' and the Overseers will rip ya' soul up out you. It's up to you if it be slow or fast. Mine left wit' daddy. But before he left, he taught me how to count, see, and 'member.

As I'm standin' on the hill, I start runnin' through my mind for things daddy taught me. Lookin' out in front of me, I 'member Massa' got fifteen slave houses. We stay in two. All the shack houses sit on top of five piles of bricks. The bricks are worn and just barely hangin' together. The pile of bricks stand 'bout a foot tall, and they got one pile under each end of the shack and three in the middle. Daddy said the Overseers made the brick piles under the shacks wide and high so they can see under the house so you can't hide. The wood used to keep the shack together is splintered and worn down. They got two cuts in the front for windows and one on each side of the shack—that way, they make sho' all the slaves where they 'posed to be. The roof barely provide cover durin' the storms.

Once a year, we get to use material to patch the roof. Sometimes we get new bricks to use on the chimney. Inside the shack, we got what we got and get to keep what they say. I 'member when we used to have two beds and three chairs, but an Overseer came and took a bed and two of the chairs when they took daddy. They said we was too comfortable and didn't deserve it. Now we left wit' just the one bed, fireplace, chair, and two blankets.

Behind the last one shack house, be the woods. So dark, not even the moon shines light down in there. Massa' house is fifty-three steps behind 'dis hill. On the left side of Massa's house is the tobacco farm, on the right is the sugar cane, on the backside is the toolin' stations and horses. Through the sugar cane side, the river be thirty-seven paces out and run all the way down.

As I feel my legs gettin' weary from standin' I step off my hill and shuffle back to the shack house. I reach for the post to help pull myself up so I can turn in like Momma said. I hear loud helpless screams in the distance with some laughin' goin' on. I turn behind me to try and gauge where the sound came from. Looks like the moon will get to see somethin' this evenin' after all. Before walkin' in the house, I step hard on the wood in front of the door to make that creak sound and say to myself, *still workin'*.

I go inside to find momma and Sam in the bed and Johnny on the floor near the fire. So I pull the chair in the corner and face towards the window, just in case.

Sat. May 07, 1831 6:15 AM: Another Working Day

"Bong! Bong!"
"Bong! Bong!"

The sound of the tower bell causes me to wake in a panic. When Ado rings the tower bell, that means ya' only got a few minutes to make it on to ya' work on time. I stand up to stretch out my overworked body. Then I walk ova' to get the rest up and ready.

"Sam... Sam! Momma! It's time. Gotta' get up." I say to them while nudging them out of their slumber. They put up the biggest fight to get up out they slumber. I guess it's their retreat to some peace. "Sam, help Momma out of bed," I say to him as I move ova to wake up Johnny-Boy.

"Okay," Sam says while stretching and rolling out of bed.

"Johnny, you bes' get movin' too!" I say to him, shovin' him awake. He shuffles 'round on the floor actin' like he don't hear me.

"Johnny! Don't stir up no trouble today, get on up now!" I demand of him. He throws the cover off himself and sits up halfway, and looks around the room. In the meantime, I walk ova' to the window to take a peek to see where the others are. We seem to be the first ones on the move. As I walk ova' to pick up Momma and my bags, I see her sittin' on the edge of the bed, rubbin' her back and knees, hummin'.

"How ya' sleep Momma?" Trying to gauge her pain level.

"I slept fine, baby. The Lawd kept' me, praise God."

Wit' my back turned to prepare our bags, I think about how in keepin' her, God didn't keep someone else last night.

I stand up to face her, smile, and say, "Well, that's good Momma."

"Reagor, come help me out 'dis here, bed, please?" asks Momma.

Gettin' his last looks at the morning sky, Sam intercedes, "I'll help ya' Momma."

"Thank ya'," Momma says to Sam as he carefully helps her to her feet.

Momma doesn't seem to be that old but has definitely done enough work fo' more than one lifetime. The ever-present threat of death ova' our heads seems to keep the body workin' from sun up to sun down. Even when the mind can't go no mo'. I stand by the door, but before I open it, I turn and look 'round at all the broken smilin' faces with pain-filled eyes ready for wat' awaits us on the other side of this door.

As the leader in this shack house, I say, "Let's go, family. Sam, Johnny, don't forget to knock on some houses before you come up." As I open the door, Johnny and Sam are the first ones out and head in different directions to go knock on some shack houses to let them know we leavin'. We learned, If some head to work sooner than others, we get other slaves in trouble, so we all in the slave quarters try to go on to work as a whole. As for me, I walk Momma slowly up the hill and head ova' to the cane fields. As we walk, she never fails to hum a tune. Me, I look at Massa' Mills house and marvel at its beauty in the Virginia mornin' sunshine.

Massa' Mills plantation be one of the biggest here in Southampton, Virginia. Massa' Mills family has 'bout 200 acres to they name. The closest plantation to us be the Whitehead plantation. The land got its own river flowin' nearby, which is why the ground we tillin' be so fertile. It capable of growin' tobacco, cotton, and sugar cane. We also not far from one of the auction ports where Massa' Mills is able to get "mo' nigger assets," as Ado like to say. By my count, they be 131 slaves livin' in the fifteen shacks here.

As Momma and me walk closer to Massa's house, out front, you see some of the older slaves tendin' to the grass, flowers, and cleanin' up the

windows of the house. Massa' house always be lookin' new every
mornin'. The tower bell sits at the top of the polished staircases wit' a
long rope fallin' down to the ground to be rung. The staircases swirl
'round on the right and left to meet in the middle, in front of the house.
I hear Massa's house got many, many rooms for the whole Mills family. I
never been in, but I can believe it when I look at that big red door. It's as
tall as two of me.

In the front courtyard, Massa' has a large raised floor that we walk
past every mornin'. On the outside of the raised floor be chairs wit'
shackles, and under each chair is a bag of salt. This be the only time we
get to sit 'round white folks. We know it as the Stage. On the right side,
be the whippin' pole side. The pole is so wide that they got to pull ya'
arms to lock you up 'round it. Before they lock you up, they strip off
some clothes before punishment. If you're really bad, they strip you
naked instead of just your back. The Overseers call it whippin' time.
Ain't no tellin' how they decide to do it, but everyday you be hearin' and
seein' a slave gettin' take down or put up there. Once done or if it's
someone else's turn, you got moved to a chair to sit and think about what
you did. On the left side, be the lynchin' post.

It really ain't a post, Massa' Mills, bein' a smart man, he made the
house tree the lynchin' tree all the slaves fear. The oak tree must be older
than Massa' Mills 'cus the roots be so thick and run so deep into the
ground it's like the life it takes goes towards given' the tree new life. It's
so strong that two people can be strung up there. Off the trunk, you see
these two large limbs twist in front like the Massa' house stairs. From
each limb hang two crimson- black blood worn, tattered nooses' cross
from each other. In case there be more than one nigger to string up, it
wouldn't be an all-day work for the Overseers. I heard one say, "It's
merciful to go hangin' side by side. A sign of my love and kindness for
you niggers."

The whippins' is so much of an everyday thing that it gets to be borin' for the Overseers to where they make us do it to one another. Lynchin' is somethin' special for 'em. They are patient and focus wit' each step. Everyone always says the rips in the tree are left behind scratches from other slaves tryin' fight they way off. There is a dark, windy piece of tree that goes all the way up. It's way darker than the rest of the tree, and there is a head- like shape at the end of the branch that hangs in the middle of the two limbs wit' nooses. When you look at the tree from a 'ways off, it almost looks like a large snake wrappin' 'round the tree. Up there to eat wat' flesh is left hangin'. At church, they say the devil is a serpent. Maybe that is him right there watchin' us hang. Massa' Mills don't take too kindly to hangin', as it is terrible for gettin' the work done. When he ends up hangin' someone, the family gots to work Sundays to buy their freedom debt. I was forced to watch a hangin' once. It was the last time I saw Sue.

Sue had run away for the third time. The last time tho' she was pregnant. When they brought her back, she was bleedin' bad from her stomach. Momma came home and told us that they caught her stabbin' her stomach wit' a stick. The doctor said she killed the baby. Massa' Mills ordered her to be hanged in the mornin' if she was still livin'. He wanted us to watch her get lynched before we went to the fields. He told us that this is the punishment for not only runnin' away but for also stealin' somethin' that wasn't hers...the baby. I still remember seein' the bright reflection off her tears as the sun shined bright on her lifeless body. She didn't fight nor shout when they were workin' on puttin' her up there. As I worked the tobacco fields that day, I thought about that. Maybe she felt that she and her baby were more safe livin' in death than livin' this life.

As Momma and I walk past, we see an Overseer gallopin' towards us fast. By the grace of God, he stops the horse before hittin' us. As the horse blows out a breath, I do the same to drudge up the energy to speak first, wit' a smile.

"Mornin', sir!" I shout to make sho' it's heard loud and clear.

"Where you headed, boy?" The Overseer states corralling his horse.

I give the answer of, "Me and Momma workin' in the cane field today, sir. Got our bags and gonna' get busy."

"Well, not today. I want you to be goin' into town wit' Ado to pick up some supplies."

"Now hurry on back there; he should be waitin' on you." He shouts down at me.

"But Sir, I gotta' get Momma to the field, and help get the work turned in. We gonna' do a real nice job out there." Tryin' to make sure Momma is safe and close so I can watch her.

The Overseer climbs down off his high horse to meet me at my place. While climbin' down slowly, he walks close to me. The closer he gets, the lower I hang my head in servitude. His presence casts a demonic shade ova' me as he starts disparaging me.

"Did you just tell me what you plan on doin'?... Are you in charge here, boy?"

"No, sir, no sir. I'd never do that there. You the boss."

"What's ya' name, boy?"

"Reagor, sir."

"Well Reagor, I suggest you get to gettin' like I told ya'. Or maybe you find ya' self laid up wit' forty lashes like Frank. I don't take too kindly to nigger talk back, you hear me, boy?"

Seein' no way out and Momma tappin' my hand to make sure I say the right thing, I respond wit', "Yes sir. I head ova' 'round back right away, sir."

The Overseer tilts his hat towards the sky to make sure I'm smilin' at his leadership. He then turns sights on Momma. While starin' at her, he makes a decree.

"Reagor, I still expect the same amount of work to get done today. I suggest you best get busy wit' ya' day, or it could end up bein' just a good day for me."

He turns 'round and gets back on his horse, and before he rides off, he warns me with, "You mind ya' self out there. We are everywhere, and we demand you niggers to follow the rules at all times."

As he rides off, I can't help but to rub and squeeze onto Momma's hand.

"It will be okay, baby. Don't fret, hear me?" She says tryin' to calm me down, grabbin' onto my face out of love.

"Now you goin' on. I'll be able to work the cane 'till you get back, and we will finish the work together, ya' hear?"

"Yes, Ma'am."

I take the bags down off my shoulder and hand 'em to her. Momma gets to shufflin' down the way towards the cane field. I steal a moment to just watch. Being a son and a slave is hard. The love I get as a son feels good but hurts 'cus I know that it can be gone at any moment 'cus all they see is two slaves, and that is all. And we will be treated like that, so time apart can become last-time if they decide. Before I get caught makin' time my time, I get to husslin' 'round back to ride into town wit' Ado.

For as far back as I can remember, Ado has always been the plantation's elected driver. Ado stood to be one of the tallest males on the plantation, tho he stands to be the skinniest one. As I make my way' round back, I stand and watch Ado strugglin' to load up the horse and wagon. I think to myself, I'm stronger than him.

What Ado lacks in strength he makes up for in hate. As the driver, he gets special treatment. His shack is right next to Massa's house. His job be drivin' the white folk wherever they want to go. If he ain't drivin' he either fixin' somethin' or plottin' somethin'. Ado believe he's better than the rest of us niggers since his color is mo' like them than us in the fields. At the end of the day, when we be comin' in, he runs off and gets to tellin' white folk about all the business we be doin'. At night I sometimes see him walkin' 'round the shack houses where the rest of us live as if he 'pose to be keepin' watch on us. The white folks did add preparin' and whippin' us to his workload.

"You just gonna' stand there nigger?! You best get to helpin' out for I tell the boss 'bout you! Have you strung up on that pole again'!"

I take a deep breath as I walk ova' and start helpin', "Yeah."

As I grab my first tobacco bag, he rushes to stand in front of me to try and tell me 'bout myself.

"It's yes Sir, boy. Don't think you goin' to be some uppity nigger 'round me now. I demands respect' round here, ya' hear me?"

Holdin' back my rage, I respond, "Yes, sir." Then I quickly walk off wit' my bag in hand to go place in the back of the wagon, movin' him in the process.

Ado stands there chucklin' and moves to pick up a bag to follow me to the back of the wagon. He starts runnin' his mouth.

"See that's that problem wit' ya'll dark niggers, thinkin' you better than everyone else when y'all some lazy dark niggers. I see y'all get up every mornin' takin' ya' time to get to work. Maybe if y'all put forth a lil' more effort and show some respect, y'all come to realize this be the Lord's will."

His words stop me dead on my way back to grab another bag.

"The Lord's will?"

"Yes, the Lord's will. See you ain't been payin' attention at church. This is how God made it to be for us. We need to sho' our gratefulness to the white man and God for all He gives us and this comfortable livin.'"

"If this is comfortable livin', then I'd hate to see what good livin' is." I respond back wit' while haulin' the last sugar cane box into the back of the wagon. When I turn my back to go take a rest in the shed, he quickly pulls me and turns me 'round and yankin' me up like I belong to him.

"See, you an uppity nigger, I'm really tryin' help you. You think you owed somethin'. Look at where you at. This life ain't yours. Just remember you dark-skin niggers ain't worth nothin' but the work you do. You best keep earnin' ya' keep 'round here and mind ya' business." He lets me go wit' a push to let that anger that's between us have some room.

"You ain't nothin'. You lower than nothin', you a nigger and don't forget that."

I decide I rather talk wit' our hands mo' than words so I shove Ado so hard he stumbles into the wagon. I stand straight up. Around white folk I hide my length, but I want this light skin nigger to know I'm not gonna' take this.

"You ain't my boss. You ain't white. Best keep to yaself, I don't care 'bout anything you talkin."

As Ado gets back up, he starts smilin' at me and responds, "You right, you right. I ain't white. But I'mma lot closer to it than you. So that makes me better than you. And I know my place too, that makes me really better than you, boy. Don't lose sight of ya' place, unless you gonna' end up like ya' Daddy."

I squeezed my fist so tight I could have broken a rock. I took a minute to look at Ado up and down, then I quickly lunged at him wit' purpose to use that fist, until we heard a distant shout.

"Hey!"

"What is goin' on back here?!"

I quickly restrain myself, let my fist go, and turn towards him as I stand silent.

"I'm talkin' to ya'll, what y'all doin' back here?!"

"Yes, Sir. Me and Reagor, just finish loadin' up the wagon for Massa' to take into town for sellin."

"Look like a couple of niggers horse playin' to me." He starts walkin' over to us wit' his hand on his hip where the whip is; easy access to dispense justice in a flash. As he gets closer, Ado and I move on out the way. He looks around and inspects the cargo in the back to make sure it's all there. Takin' his time, he gingerly walks behind us, still cuppin' his whip. He comes full circle and stands in front of us.

"Now just 'cus you back here, don't mean we can't see you. And don't mean you get to lollygag the day away." He takes a quick step to the right to be right in my face. "A nigger that ain't workin' deserves to be punished, don't ya' think?"

Full of fear, I respond softly, "Yes, Sir."

"Ado. Don't think you can get away with any 'ol thing now. You can get the same thing he gets. In fact, your comfy lil' life back here can be given to someone else, if we feel like it."

"Yes, Sir. Yes Sir. I'm sorry, so sorry."

"Good! Massa' Mills is 'bout ready to go. Pull the wagon up front for him so you can take him into town."

"Yes sir." Ado responds wit' as he gallops to the front to make sure the horse is locked in.

"Excuse me, Sir, where I'm goin' sit?"

Walkin' towards the wagon, he shoves a few of the tobacco bags towards the back and says,

"Climb in."

Hangin' my head low, I climb up and slide down slow so I can scrunch my body to fit down wit' the goods bein' sold. Once I get down, the Overseer closes up the flaps in the back of the wagon. Sittin' here in this black box back where the only light is the space between the leather surroundin' the wagon, I think to myself prayerfully, they don't sell me too. As Ado gets the horse movin' towards the front, we stop again. I see a man but can't make his face. Yet I hear Ado sayin',

"Mornin' Boss! How we feelin' today?"

11

A RIDE TO CROSS KEYS

Cross Keys was the closest town to us. Goin' into town to the market was rare for a field hand like me. We don't get to go nowhere unless we gettin' sold, beat, or workin' off Massa's debt elsewhere. I don't like the town, and it sho' don't like me. Ado finally stops the wagon, and a few minutes later, he whips back one flap.

"Get on outta' there, we got work to do," Ado shouts at me. I slowly dig myself up out of this tight spot and stumble out of the wagon. As I stop myself from fallin' in the street, I try and stand and wake up my dead legs. While I can, I look 'round the area wit' all it has goin' on. They got stores all 'round wit' pretty things to buy, the docks got the big 'ol ships wit' new arrivals comin' and stuff leavin', and they got the big 'ol barrels standin' in the "nigger spaces".

Seems like white people are made wit' nice clean clothes, shoes, and a smile. Yet I know different. Below all those smiles, glee, and fancy lives lay a shared sleepin' evil spirit in all of 'em ready to be set free at a moment's notice. There is a way of life here in America where the nigger is to be a livin' sacrifice to bring white joy, white respect, and white comfort. Any nigger thinkin', actin', or pretendin' to be more than that they can wake that spirit. Nothin' gets past the established way of life.

We know it too, where I not only had to mind my Overseers and Massa', I had to mind all Overseers and Massas. As Pastor says, "You best learn to mind the devils you know, and really mind the devils you don't."

After my stretchin', Ado signals me ova' as it's time to unload the haul. So I walk back ova' to the wagon, grab my two bags and walk it 'round behind the store. Wit' the back door open, Ado and I start puttin' the contents in, and I can't help but look into the store as I walk past. Seein' Massa' talkin', exchangin' money and laughin' wit' the other white man. Wit' each trip, I kept slowin' down by the door to get a look at Massa's face. I started to forget what he looked like; the last time I saw him close was when he was next to Daddy.

"Move it, boy! " Ado sternly says to me, tired of runnin' into me. I see Massa' lift his eyes up at us, and I immediately put my head down and walk on. Can't be caught lookin' no white man in the eye, that's the look of death.

After I grab the last sugar cane box and stack it in the backroom, I walk up to Ado tendin' to the horses.

"That there be the last one."

"Okay, good, gon' get in the back, boy. I'll tell Boss we all finished."

As I start walkin' away, Ado yells for my attention.

"Hey, boy! Thinkin' will get ya' killed. Ya' hear me?"

Puzzled by his words, as if that's somethin' I don't know. The only response I could come up wit' is, "Okay."

"You best be back there when Boss and I come out of the store."

Ado then walks towards the back of the wagon. As I'm trained to do, I climb up, sit on the floor, and wait for my Massa'. While waitin', I start thinkin' about Momma. I hope she alright, and ain't gettin' into no trouble. No sooner I start thinkin' bout Momma in trouble, a nigger came crashin' hard into the street.

Two white men came in rushin' to aid in his hurt by towerin' ova' him to kick him all ova'. He tries hard to cover his face. As they beat on 'em, I hear them say,

"You think you can laugh in front of me boy!? And what you doin' walkin' on the sidewalk!? Your place is in the street, you hear me?! I said, do you hear me?!"

They take a moment to catch their breath.

"Get up boy! Right now!"

I see him tryin' to rally 'nough strength to only turn ova' and be on all four. About now, the town has stopped to look at the dollin' out of discipline. From the safety of the wagon, I see him tryin' to get up and catch his breath, yet, 'dat breath is not his to take 'cus the two white men quickly grab him and throw him at the barrel on the corner, head first. They then pick him up and shove him inside the barrel.

"That's why these are here! You need to laugh and you can't hold it, have you a barrel! Don't ever let me see ya' sorry face out here laughin' again!"

Once they finish wit' him, I quickly turn my head 'round so they don't see me watchin'. The unknown devil is out patrollin', and I don"t wanna meet him. Out the corner of my eye, I could see them celebratin' as they skipped away makin' their lil' contribution to America count. The town stood in full agreement wit' the justice shown and went back to clean clothes, pretty things, and joy.

Ado came 'round the corner of the wagon after the yellin' was through to find out it wasn't me out here makin' trouble.

"Good, you here. We gettin' ready to go." Ado quickly shuts the flap. I survived goin' into town. As we begin to back up, when I listened close, I could hear the barrel for laughs become a barrel of tears.

Sat. May 07, 1831 8:15 PM: Shack House #2

To be the last one to turn in from the fields is a defeated feelin'. Left all alone is you and the Overseer out there watchin' ya'. Bein' a man or woman, it don't matter. You ain't safe. In fact, the Overseers delight in our fear. Livestock don't decide their fate. We just do and bend to their will.

"You finish yet, boy!?"

"Yessir. Last one right here," I say through a phoney smile.

"Good! Go turn in ya' haul at the stage and get on."

"Yessir. Bless ya', sir."

Shufflin' on back, I drop the sack of cane on the stage. Lookin' at the floor, the shadow of the rope swingin' in the breeze took my eyes. As I shift my head up, I pause and say to myself,

Always be strong.

I continue the journey back to the comforts of slavery. I see the fire be on, which means either Momma cold, or she finally got rations. I step up and walk through the door to see Sam on the floor playin' wit' rocks and Johnny-Boy sittin' in the chair lookin' out the window.

"Hey Momma, Sam, Johnny," I speak to everyone in the room.

Momma peaks her head out from the pot ova' the fire, "Hey baby, thank the Lawd you home."

"Yeah. Thank the Lawd tomorrow is Sunday. Don't have to go out in no fields." I say joyously while sittin' on the bed.

"Hey Reagor, guess what? I picked the most tobacco today!" Sam said, believin' he did something great.

"Why did you do that?" I asked.

"I don't know, I just kept pickin' until they called time. And I had the most." Sam responded.

As I slide off the bed, I start to correct him, "Sam, when you do that, you make it harder for everybody else and you. The Overseer now gonna' expect ya' to make weight like that all the time."

"Oh, I.... I didn't mean to. I just was doin' what they told me to do."

"I know. Just sometimes, we got to be sneaky in what we do 'cus we don't know what may hurt us later."

"What's wrong wit' him doin' his work? That's what he here for, right?" Johnny interrupts.

"What you mean by that? I'm not tellin' him to not work." I say.

"You tellin' Sam not to work hard. Massa' say, that's the problem. Y'all always out there bein' lazy not doin' ya' work."

I stand up from the floor to walk ova' to Johnny, starin' out the window. I swing him ova' to look me in the face.

"Hey, housework and fieldwork be different work. Don't say we don't work. We do! Hard! And I got the marks to prove it. Just 'cus you get to be in the big house, don't bring that white stuff down here."

"It's not white stuff. It's true! You just made it to be true wit' wat' you told Sam. He needs to do all he can so he can be an example for all them field niggers."

"Johnny, Reagor, stop that fightin'," Momma says tendin' to dinner while tryin' to hum ova' us.

"If I'm a nigger you one too 'cus we brothers. So you best mind me, Johnny."

"I ain't no nigger. Look at me. Look at you! I don't belong out here wit' y'all. When I get older, I'mma be up by the big house wit' Da—"

I lunge into Johnny's face and grab him by his tattered shirt hangin' low and look at him wit' all the rage I can.

"Don't ya' dare say that 'bout him! That's Massa', nothin' else. You hear me?!"

Momma comes ova' at us wit' her switch and swipes both of us on the back to where I let him go, at which she gives the final word.

"I said stop it! When I say stop, I mean, stop! Y'all hear me?!"

"Yes, Ma'am." We both answer, bendin' to her orders as Momma of the shack house.

"Johnny, go on and get supper ready."

Johnny takes his time to move on until Momma shouts at him, "I said now, boy! Get on!"

"I'm goin' outside Momma, I'm not hungry anymore." I say as I storm out and shut the door behind me.

Sittin' on the porch, I get to thinkin' 'bout Ado's words. It's troublesome when words drop down into ya' heart then into ya' spirit and start to kill both. He's right, thinkin' does get ya' killed. Thinkin' 'bout better, prayin' for a day I can take this black off me and not live this anymore is hard. You either forced to prove that you more than nothin'. More than a nigger, but I've seen and heard too many pay the price for tryin' to be more. Or you accept it. Thinkin' on the words of forever bein' a nigger and nothin' more is killin' me from the inside. To think every time I wake, I know my prayer to never wake up again gon' unanswered.

My feet begin to enjoy the relief of the fresh night rainfall hittin' 'em. Momma says rain is God cryin' over the prayers He is receivin' from us. It's hard to believe God would spend time cryin' for us instead of just helpin' us. I wish he protected Momma that night from Massa', that way, Johnny wouldn't be here causin' all this fuss in the house. I hear the soft steps comin' from inside towards me. The door opens, and it's Momma wit' a bowl in her hand.

"Hey baby, I got a bowl of suppa here for ya'."

"Thanks, Momma."

"You welcome baby, Now help me get down there wit' ya'. I wanna talk wit' ya'."

I sigh and do as I'm told. I place my arm out so Momma can slowly get down to sit by me.

"Now, I know you just 'bout a whole man and all, but I just wanna see how you doin'?"

"I'm okay, Momma... Johnny just makes me so mad sometimes."

"I know, baby, I know. He don't understand yet. Give 'em time to learn. No matter wat', he can't be one of them. He may be light, but that don't make him white. You just gotta' sho' more patience, okay?"

"Yes, Ma'am."

A pause in the conversation happens, so Momma grabs my hand and just holds it like only a mother can. I looks at her hands, holdin' mine. Despite her overburdened palms from cane work, or her ripped fingers from tobacco and cotton pickin', or welted arms from cowhide lashings, her love always seeps through. I lean my head on her shoulder and steal this moment just to live wit' Momma.

"Oh, I found out at church there gonna' be a surprise." Momma says wit' some joy.

"Oh, what is the surprise?"

"They gonna' have a travelin' speaker come down. It's a slave named Nat Turner. He has been comin' 'round to all these churches wit' his Massa' talkin' wit' slaves. They say he got God's annointin' on 'em."

"Oh, okay. That's nice Momma."

"Well, I'mma let ya' enjoy ya' suppa. Be sho' to come on to bed when you finish, we got church in the mornin'."

"Yes, Ma'am," as I help her up.

When I sit back down, I feel Momma lookin' ova' me. So I turn towards her waitin' to speak.

"Do you ever sleep?"

I turn back 'round and smile. As I'm lookin' down, I respond wit', "Sometimes."

Shakin' her head, Momma responds wit', "Lawd have Mercy. Just like ya' Daddy."

Shufflin' back to the door, Momma starts hummin'. I quickly turn back 'round.

"Hey, Momma?"

"Yes?"

"You miss him?"

She copies the smile I just gave and responds, "Everyday baby. That's why I keep hummin'. Help keep me from cryin'. Night."

As Momma heads back inside, I turn back around and stir up my suppa as the pitter-patter of my tears fall like the rain.

12

SUNDAY SERVICE - SUN. MAY 8, 1831

Sunday be the only day a slave gets a peek at freedom. On Sunday, we get to do what we want on the plantation. Some take it as a day of rest. Others take this day to tend to their wounds, sew up old clothes, or tend to the lil' crops they have to last past our rations given. Momma loves to go to church. I go for the fellowship, and I go for the distraction. There's somethin' 'bout a pastor talkin' about the Lord, brighter days, heaven, a time of rest that gives me a small idea that maybe, just maybe I'll get to know wat' it feels like. Thus far, my life has shown that life ain't somethin' for a slave, but maybe enough prayer, shoutin', and fastin' will make it happen'. Gettin' tricked wit' hope is a nice break from sufferin'.

Massa' Mills allows us to walk on over Massa' Blount's plantation next door for service. They allow the slaves to gather in the empty barnyard and get together. Most of the time, the Pastor for us is the slave of a white pastor. Next to a house nigger, they speak the best, dress the best, and even get to look at a Bible. They can't read it. They are just allowed to use it sometimes to point at stuff as if they sayin' what's inside.

Wit' daybreak in the distance, I wake everybody up so we can be dress when Ado rings the tower bell so we know it's safe to travel. Momma always puts on her Sunday best. Once a year all the women is given rations of old clothes from Massa' and his wife to turn into negro clothes. Momma saved pieces after pieces, buttons after buttons to make herself blue and checkered linen dress piece. She had a matchin' hand woven sunbonnet that she help fade into the same blue dye as the dress usin' from flowers from the fields. The pride she had in that outfit was strong. It was hers and was nothin' 'round like it. When she wore it, it was her time to be set apart from the world. A nice break when you livin' in a world that just sees a nigger woman.

"Momma we don't wanna go to church!" Johnny and Sam tryin' to defy Momma's orders, while gettin' dress.

"You may not wanna, but it's wat' you gonna' do 'cus I said so. Now get ya' selves together." Momma says sternly.

While lookin' out the window and buttonin' my shirt, I stay quiet. I don't get into that fight. To me, I can go or stay, but if it makes Momma happy, I'm willin' to do what I can. It's what Daddy did.

"Ding- Dong"

"Ding- Dong"

"Alright, boys, let's get a move on," Momma sounds off while fixin' Sam's collar.

Sat. May 08, 1831 8:30AM: Church House

There is one thing all slaves know 'bout church. The church is just 'bout the last thing that gives ya' a dose of hope. From the time ya' walk-in 'til the time you leave out, there's just a thick cloud of hope that you can't help but feel in the hot church air.

The singin' of songs, everybody clappin' their hands, the handmade drums gettin' ya' on ya' feet, the overzealous people sweatin' in their Sunday best fightin' for their turn to shout up and down the aisles. The Pastor preachin' a sermon so hard ya' soul can't help but leap up and join in on the festivities.

I'm not a believer. It's hard to believe in a God when all these people in this packed room spend all this time given' all they got left to a God for a chance to see His hand move; only to leave and be forced back into a hell full of torment, work, and fear. I think that's why service seems like it be goin' on forever. Maybe a little more time will get His attention. Me not believin' don't mean 'dis time is a waste. It is a place for us to be in peace for a spell, to rejoice our way, and how we wanna', and to be wit' our family. Sunday church service is the only place we can come together to get as much hope and joy from each other as we need to get through the days comin'.

"Brotha's and Sista's hold on to God's unchangin' hand! Wherever you be, the Lawd is wit' ya'! Believe in Him. For Christ said, serving is a good thing. So count it joy my brothas and sistas, count it joy when ya' serve. Serve to the best ya' can for ya' just reward will be given in heaven! God Bless ya'!" Shouted an exhausted Nat Turner from the pulpit at the end of his sermon.

As the congregation stood to give a standin' handclap, my eyes locked on to Nat lookin' out the window with his hand coverin' his mouth shakin' his head. It was almost as if he was unhappy wit' somethin', or perhaps he is strugglin' wit' the heat in this room as most of us do.

"Before we get ready to leave, let's bow for prayer," the Pastor asks of the saints from the front.

"Dear Lord, we thank you for this message that went out to ya' people today, Lord. Lord, we know you are wit' us, as we step out today Lawd protect us! Give us the strength Lawd to find our way and be a blessin' to 'dis here nation. Keep the Millz family, keep the Blount family, keep the Travis Family. Thank ya' for allowin' Massa' Travis to bring Nat and bless us wit' a word today. We need ya' heavenly strength Lawd, and we believe that we will see you, and the chariots will swing low for us too. In Jesus' name. And the church said?"

"Amen!"

After the prayer, Sam, Johnny, and I rush for the door to be the first ones out. Get that brisk, cool air when the doors swing wide open.

"Thank God that's ova wit'! So tired of church, I don't know why Momma makes us come," Johnny says wit' anger.

"It makes her happy, she's ya' Momma. You should wanna make her happy. Besides, what else you got goin' on that be more important?" I say, annoyed wit' him.

"Nothin', That's the point. I don't know, maybe get some time to be up 'round the big house." Johnny responds. As quickly as the words hit my ears, I turn towards him to set him straight since my words ain't doin' justice.

Sam quickly jumps in front of me and distracts my anger wit' a question,

"Reagor, Reagor, can I go play?!" Sam asks sensin' I'm 'bout to ruin everyone's happiness wit' hurtin' my brother outside the church.

I turn my eyes down towards Sam, "Yeah, go' on and play. Don't go far. We gotta' get back to the shackhouse. Don't get in no mess ya' hear?"

"Yessum!" Sam responds wit' as he runs off. Since he leaves, I decide to go' on for a walk myself instead of talkin' wit' Johnny.

As I mosey on 'round I see other slaves walk on back to their slave quarters wit' their families. Others head on back to their plantations before curfew. Keepin' on the path I'm walkin', I look up and see Nat in the distance. He's standin' behind his Massa' while he's talkin' to Massa' Blount. Tryin' not to be seen, I watch them shake hands, and Massa' Blount passes him an envelope.

"Reagor! My boy!" Pastor shouts from behind while he bear hugs me. My soul nearly leaped up out of my body. I quickly broke free to turn and face him.

"Hey Pastor, how you be?" I say as my heart calms down.

"Well, Son, well, Son. Glad to see ya' in service today. How you enjoy Nat today?"

"Just fine, just fine."

"That's good now! We glad to have him. He only gon' be up this way for awhile. He sho' is gifted wit' the word of the Lord." Pastor says happily. I just nod.

"I tell ya' boy, you lookin' more and more like ya' Daddy. Now you be sho' to let me know if you or ya' Momma need anything, alright?"

"Yes sir."

As Pastor walks off, I begin lookin' 'round for Momma and see her in the distance talkin'. Meanwhile, I quickly look up as I see the shadow under me grow. Since the sky is as still as ever, it looks like there won't be an answer from God, I decide I best be walkin' 'round to collect Sam, Johnny, and Momma to head on back to the shackhouse. Prayerfully Momma will start on suppa'.

13

CHOICE IS DANGEROUS- SUN. MAY 8, 1831

Sunday nights be 'da worst. I lay up rockin' in my chair wit' my shirt coverin' my knockin' knees from the cold, I can't help but just stare at the distant sky.

Wonderin'...

Wonderin', why me? why my family? why us?....

Wat' could we have done to be different to not be here? I look ova' and see Momma holdin' Sam in her arms in the bed. She's so tired. I wish I could just give her rest. Give her peace. I look down at Johnny curled up on the floor near the fireplace. I come to realize that he's changin'.

This life is causin' a change in him and I know 'cus it already done caused a change in me and right now we ain't seein' things the same anymo'. We no mo' than a few steps apart, but the paths we are forced on is pullin' us worlds apart. The more he gets 'round that house, the more he takes after Ado. Can I blame him for that? A house nigger is still a nigger, so choices ain't his to make.

I want to love him, but wat' he be... whose he be... and who I am don't mix.

"BAM!"

The echo from the sound run through me so quick, it got me to leap right out the chair. Collectin' myself, I get my footin' and lissen' hard.

Slowly, I walk ova' to the fire stove and grab the empty dinner pot. Whatever is out there, I can't afford to let it come in here. 'Dis time I'm old enough to fight if need be. As I stand holdin' the pot, I stare at the front door for what feels like forever only for nothin' to happen. Wit' every passin' moment the pot's weight in my hand gets heavier, and my heart starts racin' faster and faster. After forever and a second goes by, I decide to meet my fear behind the door. Slowly I begin to march towards the door, when I make it to the front, I swing open the door to be met by the night silence.

I walk out front to look 'round and make sure my fear wasn't 'round the corner. As I look to my left and right wit' no danger in sight, a calm rushes ova' me to place my spirit back at ease.

"Thank God." I utter silently as I let off a deep sigh. As I turn 'round to head back inside I hear a patter of feet shuffle in the distance which wakes up my senses again. I quickly turn and peek back over my shoulder and look for the sound.

In the distance, near shacks eight, nine, and ten I see slaves... runnin'.

"Oh my God, are they runnin'? Where are they goin'?"

As I watch 'em in the distance, the three of 'em run off 'tween the shacks then dart for the woods. My mind can't help but wonder where they think theys goin'. No runaway lasts mo' than three days before bein' dragged back. Massa' makes sho' runaways get dealt wit'.

As I see them disappear off into the woods, I shake my head knowin' there is goin' to be hell to pay tomorrow if they get found. I walk back and reach for the door only to stop. Almos' like my mind won't let my hand go to grab fo' the door.

Captivated by the question, *where they goin'?*

Seein' some slaves run off you gotta' think 'bout the strength it takes for them to make a choice like that. That's... dangerous!

I just watched some slaves try livin' they life before my very eyes.

What does that feel like? Can I do that? Do I want to do that?

My mind lets my hand fall. I slowly turn 'round. I take a step off the porch. I take another step down the hill and stand. Silence.

I take two more steps...

Only forty-seven more steps to the woodline, I think to myself. No sooner than I think it, my feet start movin'! Faster and faster my feet go, my mouth curls, the wind is hittin' my face like I'm burstin' through a clear wall to get to where I want to go!

Baskin' in this sensation of choice, a genuine smile comes ova' my face. I think, *I did it! I did it!*

Hunched ova', takin' in some air after runnin', I listen for sounds of trouble to meet me only to hear my deep breaths bein' masked by the evening wind. I look out into the woods and see a sheet of darkness.

"Where they go?" I say to myself as I stand up, recovered from my run. Before turnin' 'round, I wait a minute to listen out for anythin'.

"SPLASH!" "SPLASH!" "SPLASH!"

I wait, and then again I hear…

"SPLASH!" "SPLASH!" "SPLASH!"

I perk up, "That was close! They must be near the water!"

I give it some time, hear silence in front of me, and silence behind me. Then I's figure. I's figure I come 'dis far and the water is not far away…

"PITTER-PATTER" "PITTER-PATTER"
Silence.
"PITTER-PATTER" "PITTER-PATTER"
Silence.
"PITTER-PATTER" "PITTER-PATTER"
Silence.

This was the safety pattern I repeated for wat' seemed like forever!

Reagor, turn back! You gon' die out here! I think to myself in the silence. After each one, I keep goin' farther, deeper into the dark woods until finally, I hears the waves of the river to the left. They don't sound like the splashes I heard earlier; they sound normal now. I take a couple more steps to get closer, my worry gets stronger, thinkin', maybe they gone, and I'm too late.

"Lord, keep the sun asleep long enough for me to make it home to Momma," I think to myself marchin' straight only to take a tumble!

Wit' every roll, the rustlin' of tree limbs brakin' and leaves cracklin' gets to be a symphony of sounds for the world to hear and find me. After the third tumble, I slam against a big tree. Usin' the tree for support, I tries to get to back to my feet. As my hands go up the tree, I start to feel somethin' strange. If I didn't know better, I'd say this was a wet blanket hangin'. The more I feel, the more right I be. There is a wet blanket hangin' up in the woods.

As I'm feelin' on this wet blanket, somethin' in the night whiffs the blanket away, grabs, and pulls me through the blanket to the other side. As I gettin' pulled through somethin' grabs my other arm and my covers my mouth.

I think to myself, *It's ova'! Why I did this?!*

Unable to wrestle free, I start to look hard into the dark at which I see the people that are holdin' me are some niggers. Then I look straight, and there are eight mo' in a circle. As I set aside my fear of death, I realize that the one in front is Nat.

14

BEHIND THE CURTAIN - SUN. MAY 8, 1831

"Reagor? Reagor, is that you boy?"

The hand coverin' my mouth moves to let me answer, "Yes sir." I respond, not really makin' out any other faces just locked in on Nat's eyes, which I can tell are decidin' what to do wit' me.

"It's me, Isaac. Did you follow us out here?"

I turn my head to face Isaac and answer, "Yes sir. I saw you and some others run off in 'da woods."

"Yes. Ms. Marry Ann and Catherine are here."

Isaac turns to Nat, "I'm sorry, I didn't know he saw us. He's a young boy. He don't know no better."

"How you find us?" Nat asks.

"I heard the splash in the water." I say.

Nat gets off his knees and walks ova' to me and says, "You gonna' tell what you seen here?"

Captive by the strength in his eyes, "No, sir. No sir. I... I just wanna go 'on back to my momma."

Nat breathes in and out. "Sit."

The two men holdin' me help me down next to 'em. I look 'round tryin' to make out wat' is happenin'. More importantly, will they let me live?

Nat sits back down in the circle. He then begins to talk.

"The God, the real and livin' God is wit' us. He won't have us suffer for much longer. These false prophets will be handled!"

As I look on, he digs in what looks like a satchel, pulls out a book, and waves it.

"This is wat' they don't want us to have, the real word of God! Here it says they are of their father the devil. They don't want it to be true, so they teach us this false word to make us work more, to not live, not be who we are. I tell you, continue to believe, continue to teach ya' friends 'bout the real God."

"To me, belongeth vengeance and recompense. They foot shall slide in due time, fo' the day of their calamity is at hand, and the things that shall come upon them make haste. God has shown me a vision, and that day is soon to come where we will see His vengeance come and deliver us. They shall fall, and we will live. One way or another, be ready to come together fo' the Lord will move just as He did fo' the Jews."

I listen to Nat teach and preach again, but this was different. The Nat' 'dis mornin' was 'bout servinin', this Nat, he talkin' bout somethin' different. He talkin' 'bout stuff that can get us killed. Lookin' in his eyes, there is somethin' different. This message, He believes.

As they end in prayer, Nat walks over to me.

"Hark, Henry, 'gon head back. 'Member to take down the tent. Let me talk to Reagor."

The two men beside me said yes sir and began pullin' down the blankets hangin'.

"Wat' them blankets for?" I ask. Hopin' to distract him as I plot to escape.

"Wet blankets keep the sound in. It's the only way we can have real service."

"Real service?"

"Yes. Real, do you know what 'real' means?"

"No sir."

"It means, tellin' the truth... bein' honest. Understand?" Nat says. I nod my head to agree.

"They fear you hearin' 'bout the real God. Maybe if you know, you may become what the white man fears. Do you know wat' that is?"

"No sir."

"You becomin' a human. And even worse, a human wit' a mind and power. That same power that led you out here. Not many slaves would come. Wasn't you scared?"

"Yes sir."

"Yet, you came anyway?"

"Yes sir. Even tho' I was scared, the more I went, the better I was feelin'."

Nat looks me up and down and strokes his chin.

"I saw you lookin' at Massa' Joseph Travis and me."

"Yes sir."

"Massa' Travis, he is makin' money off the gospel. He sends me 'round to tell slaves to continue to work hard for they Massa'."

"Why you do it?"

"Cus for now, he is my Massa'. I'm waitin' for my other Massa' to tell me to stop and fight."

"You talkin' 'bout God?"

"Yes sir."

"Well, I don't think that happenin'. God is just like them, so I don't see Him carin' 'bout helpin' a bunch of niggers."

Nat briefly smiles and responds to my tone, "Well if He gives you the tools to fight, would ya'?"

"I don't know."

"Help may come in a way you not ready fo', but if ya' keep ya' eyes open, maybe you'll see it. Like you saw Isaac and 'em."

"In seven days, we gon' be back out here. Come."

"Why?"

"You just might see that help."

15

Nat Comin' Into A Purpose - Fri. Dec. 02, 1825

Faster, Nat, Faster... Just a lil' farther... Just a lil' farther!

Is the only thought playin' ova' and ova' in my spirit. I think to myself as I'm escapin' for freedom, "No mo' can I bear this life. No mo' can I live like 'dis here."

The cold winter night sky looks ova' me as I'm dashin' up and through the dense Virginia woods. I do my best to make my pace match the heavy snowfall, hopin' its keeps comin' down hard enough to cover my footprints. Wit' each breath, I make a step. Wit' each step I get that much further away from them chains and that much closer to somethin' I never had, freedom. As I'm tearin' through tree limbs and jumpin' ova' snow-covered logs and bushes in my way, all I keep thinkin' is, "Keep headin' for freedom."

The feelin' of freedom is all I care 'bout.

These scratches on my hands won't stop me. My frozen bare feet stumblin' through this ankle-high snow feels lighter than the shackles I've worn all my life. Not even my bleedin' wounds on my back can slow me down. Open bloody wounds for a slave is like the sun, you can always count on them bein' there if it's mornin'. The only thing my mind can focus on is...

Faster Nat, faster... Just a lil' farther... Just a lil' farther! You can do it, Nat!... Run through it... Run through it!

No sooner than I thought it, my body suffered for that choice. Not seein' what's on the other side of that bush, I ran myself right off the hillside cliff.

Not knowin' which way is up, I now a slave to the fall off the hillside. Again, stripped of my choices, gravity is choosin' which way to throw me and how hard to throw me. All I could wonder wit' every passin' tumble is, will this be how I get caught?

Wit' no pity fo' me the hillside flings my body sideways so hard into a fallen tree fo' a moment, I thought death decided to take my hand. Dare to dream.

Lyin' across the log, I manage enough strength to turn ova' and slide down to look at the trail left behind from my fall. Holdin' on to my side, I sit in the still of the night watchin' my negro breath mix wit' the pure white snowfall. As time passes, I realize death isn't at the top of the hill carryin' dogs, so I slowly stagger to my feet, hopin' it helps me breathe better.

As I'm holdin' my right side as if it's a sucklin' baby, I try my best to stand tall wit' no luck. Every gasp has some pain followin' right behind it. Finally, I say all soft,

"God, I can't do this!"

"God! You hear me?! I can't do this anymo'... If you is real, God, take me on up to glory or let me die right here."

"God, I've seen so much pain. So much hurt wit' no peace on the way. My heart can't take bein' done wrong no mo'. Wit' every whippin' I see, every scream I hear, I feel their pain. Please, Lord, let me escape to freedom, and I'll at least be safe for my body and soul to heal up to where I can come back to get my people out."

After my complainin' my body came to enough to where I could get back on the move. I slowly slid my body across the log to get to the other side. As I head back into the woods, I looked 'round for the safest way possible. Decidin' to go to the left, I began to climb ova' the small bushes only to make it a few good steps onward 'til I fell to my face. Pickin' myself up and slingin' the snow and mud off my face, I look back to see what had caused my fall only to see what looked to be an empty sack bag.

Filled wit' anger, I gave the bag a tug, come to realize it's buried. I furiously start shovin' back dirt and rocks out the way. Finally, I was able to pull the bag out the ground. Once I untied it, I put my hand inside and pulled out a small black tattered book. As I began to look through it, I realized it's a Bible. Completely distracted from my reason for bein' out here, I think to myself, why would someone bury 'dis Bible? And somethin' happened that never happened to me before, I heard from God.

The clouds parted to where the moon was shinin' right on me and the only page I could read,

"Servants, be obedient to them that are your masters according to the flesh, with fear and trembling, in singleness of your heart, as unto Christ;"

Wit' new energy, I rose to my feet in anger!

"Wat' you sayin', Lord! I need to go back!? I'm 'posed to like this life and dwell in it?! No! I won't, I'm not acceptin' this! Do you hear me?!"

My anger was met wit' the dead of the night silence. Only the shimmerin' moonlight remained.

"Do you see wat' this life here is doin' to us?!" More than angry, I'm hurt. "Lord, a mother shouldn't have to kill her own chil'ren to believe that they are mo' safe to suffer once than have them grow up in slavery and be murdered piece-meal!... Then to find herself hung for taken the life of property she didn't own. Father, I still feel Peggy's blood splash up against my face when they cut her head off. Why must we find comfort in sufferin' and look towards death as a chance at life? I've come to accept you, and this is how I'm shown care? Is this how all us slaves are shown favor? Slavery ain't no gift!"

As I march ova' to pick up the tattered Bible, wit' tears coursing down my cheeks, I say out loud so God could hear, " 'Dis here is wat' I think of ya' Word!" I gripped the Bible to tear out the page. Right when I was 'bout to start pullin', my eyes got hold of somethin' I never saw before.

"And, ye masters, do the same things unto them, forbearing threatening: knowing that your Master also is in heaven; neither is there respect of persons with him."

As the weight of those words hit me, I felt a strong breeze blow through me. As if the breeze was the breath of God fillin' my body.

I felt a change.

I closed the book, placed it back in the bag. I closed up the bag, put it ova' my shoulder, took a deep breath to get to my feet, and went on the path I left behind.

As I sneak back into my shack, I relight the fire to sit next to it to get some warmth and dryness. Sittin' next to the fire, I just stare at the battered bag, I'm too scared to open it again. Scared to see if my mind played tricks on me to stop me from gettin' wat' I been wantin'. Once my hands are warm enough to move, I go ova' to open it.

Sho' nuff, the words were still there in the book. I quickly turn it to the front to read the cover and the 'Holy Bible' is what it said. As I put it down, I turn the satchel upside down, come to find there's more inside. I pull out bundles of paper. The first bundle cover reads:

Testament of Denmark Vessey:
"I, Denmark Vessey of sound mind, and wishin' to provide someone my will and testament before my death come. I make this my will and testament to aid a fellow negro able to find and use my words.
To Writ under my hand this 10th day of June 1822

The next bundle cover read:
Testament of Gabriel Pressor:
"I, Gabriel Pressor of sound mind, and wishin' to provide someone my will and testament before my death come. I make this my will and testament to aid a fellow negro able to find and use my words.
To Writ under my hand this 21st day of September 1800

The next bundle cover read:
Testament of Charles Deslondes:
"I, Charles Deslondes of sound mind, and wishin' to provide someone my will and testament before my death come. I make this

my will and testament to aid a fellow negro able to find and use my words.

To Writ under my hand this 07th day of January 1811

As I sit by the fire, lookin' at everythin' on the floor I couldn't help but feel somewhere in all this, there be an answer to my questions and a way out. Just gotta' put it together.

Sat. May 13, 1831 10:30 PM: Reagor's Shack House

One of the biggest reasons you can catch a whippin' or floggin' is if the Overseers hear some talk you ain't supposed to be havin'. They job is to keep us busy wit' work, but more than that if they hear anythin' 'bout freedom that will get you five lashes right then and there in the field. Like fightin' smallpox, any hint of it, and they must destroy it unless it's able to spread, and I see why.

All week I been thinkin' heavy 'bout wat' Nat said this past Sunday in the woods. Bein' mo than a slave, become a human. All my life, all I saw a slave was, was a slave. I thought of us as only slaves. There was no thinkin' past that to us bein' thought of as a people.

Workin' in the fields this week, I was seein' these Overseers just bein' who they wanna to be. They's had freedom since birth and a will they could use that I couldn't. Yet, now that I knows that, it's all I fearfully want.

Sittin' outside while everybody else sleepin' their night away, I oversee the fight in my mind between goin' for freedom and the dangers between me and freedom. Imagin' wat' I can be by havin' my freedom versus wat' white people gon' do to stop me from havin' freedom. Nat said startin' to imagine, and hope is you tastin' a bit of freedom. To be fully free and become wat', they fear it's goin' to take strength. Daddy told me to always be strong, but Daddy bein' strong is how he gots himself killed.

I think 'bout why I can't feel, and I know it's 'cus ever since they killed him, all I feel is hate. All I see is his death.

It was 'bout eight summers ago. I remember Ado rang the tower bell just like any other day, and Daddy got us all up and ready to go. I was able to sleep in the bed wit' Momma, Johnny slept in Daddy's lap in the chair, and Jimmy slept on the floor since he was too big. Sam was in Momma's stomach. Jimmy and I wanted to be like Daddy. We always got to work wit' him.

Before we left, Daddy would kiss us all as we went out da' door and said, "Be strong today."

As we headed up the hill to go to the fields, the Overseer rounded us slaves in front of the big house. Massa' Mills was standin' on the raised floor where he was, started talkin' to us.

"My niggers, as you can see, there is a bunch of chil'ren runnin' 'round here. While that's a good thing in y'all makin' more workers for me, I can't keep feedin' y'all. So wat' we gonna' do is round up some of these kids to get them sold off," Massa' Mills said.

As he said it, some Overseers came up behind the slaves as others stood in front. Then goin' thru one by one they started snatchin' up kids. As they began, the mountainous cries and shoutin' followed. Daddy stood closer to Momma and pushed Jimmy and me behind them.

I still see Daddy's hand squeeze tighter, and we all were seein' kids bein' snatched from they mommas and daddies.

"Hey! Now stop this now! This is gon' happen one way or the other!" Massa' Mills yelled at us, as Overseers were pickin' and choosin' which kids to snatch.

"Move." An Overseer standin' in front of Daddy said.

First lookin' at the ground, I saw Daddy slowly raise his head to look a white man in the eye and said, "No." Never have I seen a slave like my Daddy and stand up to white folks fo' his heart, his family. Not standin' for this, the Overseer took the butt of his gun and hit Daddy in the face screamin',

"Nigger, I said move! Get out my way! And who do you think you lookin' at boy?! I'll rip ya' damn eyes out if you ever look at me again!" The Overseer shouted towerin' over Daddy. As Daddy was on one knee, he did the unthinkable. He made a choice.

"Ahhh!!" Daddy unleashed a scream from his soul and exploded up wit' that clinched fist hittin' the Overseer in da' face causin' him to fall on the ground. Followin' him to the ground, Daddy jumped on top of 'em strikin' him as many times as he could before gettin' toppled from behind by two other Overseers. Even then Daddy was fightin' wit' all 'dat was in 'em.

Momma pulled so hard on my arm to keep me next to her. Once she had me, she reached out for Jimmy only to see him run and jump on the back of an Overseer.

"No! Jimmy! Get back ova' here!" Momma cried out.

It's too late, the Overseer in the back ran up and yanked Jimmy by his oversized stretched shirt and threw him to the right, where Jimmy fell to the ground. He came ova' and rests his foot on Jimmy's back to keep 'em still on the ground.

"Get him up! Get him up now!" Massa' Mills shouted at the Overseers that were stompin' Daddy into the ground. They soon after stopped and dragged him to his feet.

By this time, all the slaves have retreated back from the scene of the crime yet not runnin' away for fear they'd had got caught up in this mess. Momma was clutchin' onto me tight to where I could barely breathe.

On each side of Daddy, he had two Overseers holdin' him still, facin' Massa' Mills.

"Boy, what you thinkin' about attackin' a white man, have you lost ya' mind?!" Massa' Mills shouted.

"You not takin' my boy!"

"Your boy?! You don't have a 'boy 'round here! These kids belong to me! YOU belong to me, you hear me, boy!?"

All I heard was the distant birds chirppin' and the pitter-patter of Daddy's blood drippin' from his face onto the dusky dirt. Watchin' from a distance, you see Daddy started to breathe slower, his arms comin' calm. He breathed out loud, for all to hear.

Slicin' through the air in the distance, you saw somethin' red slam hard against Massa' Mills face. Takin' a minute to know'd wat' just happened, Massa' Mills jumped down to kick Daddy in his chest, knockin' him back onto the ground.

"Nigger! You spit on me! Who do you think you are!?" Massa' Mills shouted.

As the Overseers picked 'em up, they asked, "You want us to hang 'em?"

Wipin' his face wit' disgust that this nigger blood had tainted his pureness, "Not yet."

Grabbin' Daddy by his hair, Massa' pushed Daddy's head back as far as he could, almos' breakin' his neck. He then said, "Strip him and flog him. His 'boy' too," Massa' Mills turned to face us slaves cowerin' and yells, "they goin' to be yo' example in learnin' that yo' life is what I say it is!"

For the next three days, Daddy and Jimmy were heard screamin'. I would sneak out at night to try and see 'em from my hill, but I couldn't. There's nothin' I could do but hear their cries. I would cry along wit' 'em. The fourth mornin' all the slaves got called up. Lookin' up there, I couldn't hold my tears. I knowed that's Jimmy and Daddy, I could'nt tell 'cus they faces and bodies had been beatin' so bad. Both of 'em rested shackled naked to they chairs. They bodies looked to be swollen 'cus they covered in salt. Some got washed off by the streams of blood comin' from the open wounds.

Momma kept on tryin' to turn me so I could'nt see, but I wanted to see... I needed to see it.

An overseer bringed a steel foot tub wit' some water in it and puts it on the raised floor.

"A few days ago, we had an incident that happened right here." Massa' Mills said to the slaves gathered as he made his way up.

"This buck nigger forgot his place and decided to not do what I had told him to. He thought he could cross the line and save his 'boy', forgettin' that he don't have sons. He don't have a life... His and your sole purpose on this God-given earth is to do what the hell I tell ya' to do!"

As he walked ova' to Daddy and faced him wit' bound hand and feet, he continued,

"Then this savage decided to do the unthinkable. He spat on me. Tried to defile my body wit' ya' evil. Clearly, you have lost all sense of value to me, so I must use you as an example for the other niggers 'round here."

"String him up! Unshackle the boy." Massa' Mills commanded.

The Overseers followed his orders as Massa' Mills puts on some gloves. They bound Daddy's hands behind him and kept his feet in shackles. They stood him up on a chair so they place the noose 'round his neck. Once they put him up, Massa' tells the Overseers to turn Daddy towards him.

There behind the tub was Jimmy. Clingin' fo' life, he's was on his hands and knees. Massa' Mills was crouched behind 'em.

"Since you thought your life and your son's life was worth savin', I want you to see how much I care 'bout your son before you go 'on to glory, boy."

Wit' crimson rushin' through his body and a drunken rage in his eyes, Massa' shoved Jimmy into the tub head first. Momma shouted out from her soul,

"NO! Massa' No!!"

"Shut up! You shut it up right now! Or you'll be next!" he screamed at Momma. Turnin' back at Daddy, he delightfully shouted, "kick the chair!" The Overseers did just that..

Momma had me clutched into her so that I couldn't see. All I felt was her drum pounding heart racin', the steady rain of tears, and her helpless grip keepin' me close. I hear'd the tree shakin' 'round. Massa' shouted,

"You watchin' boy?!"

"Ya' boy needs ya'... come on and get him! Save him!"

The tusslin' of the tree limbs started to dwindle wit' time...

"Hey nigger, How's it hangin'?"

No mo' tree tusslin'. No mo' water splashin'.

All was quiet.

Momma fell limp to the ground face first, wit' me underneath her. I dug my way from under her and got to my feet. I looked at her laid out on the unforgivin' Virginia soil. The weight of this moment had broken her. All she was able to do wit' out stretched arms, was cry and hum. Hummin' and cryin'. Hummin' and cryin'. I slowly turned my head to look up and see the stillness on stage.

Be strong... Be strong.

Ugh! Get it together! I say to myself explodin' up on the porch tryin' not to focus on my hurt but on the choice I need to make.

"Chirp -Chirp.... Chirp -Chirp... Chirp-Chirp" echoes through the slave quarters. It's time to meet.

16
TOO PURPOSED. I'M TIRED. - FRI. MAY 13, 1831

"Men and Women. Ya' courage to come here tonight tells me a lot 'bout who you are and ya' will to do somethin'. I thank ya' for believin' in me enough to risk ya' lives just to hear wat' the Lord has to share." Nat shares from his heart.

Listenin' to Nat speak is a feelin' I never get elsewhere. The words he says, the way he moves, his belief is fallin' on me. Ya' look up and ya' blood gets warm, ya' feel a feelin' you ain't never felt. Ya' feel true hope. Nat keeps on speakin',

"Some time ago, I ran for freedom. I was hopin' to leave it all behind. The Massas', the work, and the fear. I was gonna' leave y'all in bondage behind. The Lord wrestled me and made me come back. For months the negroes 'round me laughed, sayin' I was a fool for comin' back. The way they treated me, I sho' 'nuff felt like one. Durin' an end to my fast, the Holy Spirit placed me in a deep sleep to have a vision and to speak two things to me. That's wat' I'm here to share wit' ya' and been sharin' across my travels wit' my Massa'. The vision I had was of white and black spirits in a bloody battle. The battle was long. At different times the white spirits would be winnin', then the black spirits would come up and start winnin'. Then quickly, the sun witnessin' darkened, and blood started flowin' in streams."

His dream excites the congregation. A woman in the circle starts to tear up. Another man starts pacin' back and forth. Finally, a woman in the back shouts,

"So wat' this mean for us?!"

Nat quiets the crowd so that he can speak,

"There's mo', and then I'll tell ya' exactly wat' it means for us. After the vision, the voice of the Lord said, 'Such is your luck, such you are called to see, and let it come rough or smooth you must surely bare it. Speak the true gospel, for the cries of ya' people have been heard. Those who hear the truth will come forth to do the will of the Lord. When I call, follow, and I will bless the hands."

"Brothas and Sistas, the cries, blood, and prayers of our people have not gon' in vain. The white man's false teachings have tainted our spirits long enough, and the Lord seeks to deliver us. He brought me back so that I might lead us into battle for freedom."

"Wat!?... Ya' want us to fight them?!... We will sho' 'nuff die!... We lucky we ain't gettin' killed right now for bein' out here!" the crowd responds to the call. In the back where I am, I'm just takin' in all that's happenin'.

"Look! Now, look! On Sundays, when I'm here, y'all listen to me speak to get a word. That word is from the white lies! That is not the truth! Just like you, my Massa' has abused me and used me. This here tonight, wat' I share is the real word from the Lord. We are all not called to this fight, the few that are, it is our responsibility to fight, and the Lord said he will be wit' us. True freedom is given to those who are willin' to fight for those that can't."

"Now I don't know when we will begin yet, but I will. Fo' those that will fight when the time comes, let us be ready. Let's gon' break to get back home." Nat concludes all wit'.

One by one, the crowd leaves 'till all that's left is me, Nat, and six others. As I'm walkin' ova', I see Nat smile.

"Men. This here is Reagor. Reagor, this here is Jack, Will, Henry, Hark the Herc, Nelson, and Sam."

'Round they all go shakin' my hand. After which Nat has me to join in on the talk.

"Reagor, we here are havin' a problem. We tryin' to do our best to spread the word 'bout the upcomin' rebellion. We need to be smart 'bout who and when we tellin' people 'bout it."

Nelson says, "Yes! Can't trust all the niggers out here."

"Negroes. Nelson, it's negroes." Hark harshly corrects Nelson.

"Look, I said wat' I said. Now I'm here, ain't I? Let's not fight 'bout this here and now!"

Watchin' this, they sounds like Johnny-Boy and me. Nelson by his look I'm guessin' he a house nigger. Hark, he gots to be a field nigger. Wit' his arms as big as trees and nearly the height of two niggers, he be wat' they call a black buck.

"Men, stop. We gotta' get back on track here. Massa' Travis and me leave fo' the next few months before we come back to Virginia. We need to know."

"Are all y'all from different plantations?" I ask.

Henry says, "Nat and I from the same, Nelson and Hark from the same, Will from olda' Massa' Francis, Jack and Sam belong elsewhere."

"Is y'all field hands?"

"Naw. Nat be preachin' and workin' wit' the tools outback. I'm in the fields. So be Will and Sam. Nelson is a driver, Jack is in the house..."

"I be a blacksmith and field hand," Hark spews.

I look up at the sky for a moment. I feel them lookin' at me while I'm thinkin'.

"You got an idea or somethin' boy?" Nelson spews at me.

"When ya'll go into town, how 'bout ya'll make use of the barrels that be fo' the niggers? Y'all just stick ya' heads in wit' others that ya' know or trust and spread the word."

"You want us to wat'?! How would that work?" Hark asks.

Nat follows up Hark's question wit', "That's exactly wat' we will do. It lets y'all talk to other slaves you know without gettin' in trouble. That way, we can have less meetings like 'dis at night!"

Nat looks at me, "Good Reagor. Very good."

"Okay all, let's go on back, don't need anyone gettin' caught and dyin.'"

As I shake my head and turn 'round to sneak back home. I feel a tug on my arm.

"Hey, let me talk wit' ya" Nat says.

I turn 'round and see the rest leave. I turn back and see Nat sittin' on a log, holdin' his Bible. Waitin'.

My heart starts racin' like a rabbit. I don't know why, but Nat scares me, yet I want to be 'round him. I mean... he's the reason I came out here in the first place. I take a deep breath to calm my heart and take a seat on the stump 'cross from him. All he doin' is tossin' his Bible back and forth, lookin' at the ground. At least the silence helps to make sure ain't no one else 'round.

"How old is you, Reagor?" Nat asks.

"My Momma say about eighteen or nineteen winters."

"Got any brothas or sistas?"

"Two brothas now."

"Ya' daddy still 'round?"

"No sir."

"Sold? Runaway?"

"They hung him for tryin' to save my older brotha and hittin' a white man."

Nat looked at me and nodded.

"Can you read?"

"I can count. My daddy taught me how to count real good."

"That's good, that's good. You know wat' that tells me?"

"Wat' sir?"

Pointin' at his head, "You not afraid to use ya' mind. Most negroes have been taught not to think, to be scared to think. Thinkin' and learnin' can get you killed as a slave. To the whites, they think it can poison a slave's mind."

"Poison?"

"Yes, like to make sick up in ya' head wit' thoughts."

"Wat' kind of thoughts?"

"Thoughts of bein' mo'. Thoughts of knowin' truth and not believin' lies. Most of the time, they use this to lie to themself and to us." He shares wit' me while holdin' up the Bible.

"Yeah that's why I don't believe in God. My Momma does, and you do, which is fine. I just don't know. Wit' wat' I've seen, it be hard to believe." I share.

"You ever heard of Joseph?"

"No sir."

"He was a boy, sold off by his brothas to Egypt to be a slave. While a slave, he learned how to read and write his Massa's language. He also used his thoughts. That slave grew up and became a leader over Egypt."

"Sounds like someone tellin' a story to me. Ain't no slave becomin' a leader." I says.

"Why not? All you need is the tools, right? You use tools to work. Why not use tools to become somethin'? Just like Joseph, my first owner used this book to teach me how to read. Never did they let me know about these stories' thou 'till I found this."

I didn't know wat' to say, so I let my silence talk. After a while, Nat spoke again,

"You know I see somethin' in ya' Son, somethin' you ain't seen in yaself. You already thinkin' and usin' ya' thoughts. That's good. Would you like to learn how to read?"

I nervously says, "I don't know." 'cus the fear of bein' out here too long is startin' to creep up.

"Fear can make things scary, especially since you and I could die if we got found. We can die for wat' we doin' now or even for wat' we know. I could get hung for havin' this here book. I choose to start bein' in power so they can be in fear and not me be in fear. If you start takin' that power, you won't be so bound by fear. You'll be consumed wit' choices."

Nat stands up and walks ova' to me, and sits on the ground.

"So I ask again, you want to learn how to read?"

As he waits for my answer, my leg starts to jump up and down. My insides startin' to get hot and feel that feelin' I felt the last time I made a choice.

"Yes sir."

Tues. July 26, 1831 09:30PM: Shack House #2

"Really pourin' out tonight, huh?"

"Reagor?"

"Boy!" Momma shouts at me as she hit me in the chest.

"Huh?! I'm sorry. You say somethin' Momma?" I says.

She puts her hand on her hip and says, "Boy, what's on ya' heart that's got ya' attention?"

"Oh, nothin' Momma I was... I was just enjoyin' sittin' here wit' ya' lookin' at the rain. I was just lost in the sound of the rain, that's all."

"Mmhm, sure. You know you can't fool me, boy. I birthed ya'. I know when somethin' is on ya' mind and I know when somethin' is on ya' heart. Come on, talk to me."

I look down at the ground watchin' the mud splashin' up on to my feet and ankles from the heavy rainfall. I couldn't hide from Momma no matter how hard I try. Knowin' there's no way 'round it, I decide to confess.

"I don't know Momma. I just think 'bout Daddy and Jimmy a lot. I wonder wat' it would be like if Daddy was still here... maybe I'd be better... know better."

"Baby, you doin' just fine. I thank the good Lawd fo' you every day! You remember wat' ya' Daddy'd say every mornin' before work?"

"Yessum." I answer wit' a smile, "Be strong!"

She smiles back at me, "Yes! Be strong. That was God speakin' through that man. He knew we needed that way down in our spirit. Reagor, you been just that fo' me, for ya' brothers, and for yaself."

I look up at Momma to see some tears of joy.

"Even lately, you've been actin' different. You been standin' tall and been 'bout ya' work. That's why I figure you been so tired."

I look off and then quickly respond wit', "Yes, that the reason."

"You been exactly wat' ya' Daddy expected of ya'."

"Thank ya' Momma. Do ya' think 'bout him?"

"Everyday I get up and out that bed. He ain't never gonna' leave my heart, nor Jimmy. I sing them a song everyday, all day, to let them know

I'm thinkin' of 'em. I's grateful the Lawd gave me a great man. I know he's gettin' his rest and Jimmy too."

"Jimmy was such a good boy. Carin', happy... He loved bein' ya' older brotha. He always wanted to be wit' ya'. Ya' Daddy told him you was his responsibility and he took it to heart. He was love."

"Yeah... I loved havin' an older brotha."

Even for a slave, there are moments if ya' try hard enough. If ya' push 'gainst the rules, you can find moments of peace. Have moments for love that can just make ya' feel like ya' worth somethin'. Like ya' more than somethin' but you is someone to somebody.

"I'mma go 'on to bed now. Goodnight, baby." Momma says as she leans on me to get up to her feet from sittin' on the porch.

"Momma?"

She stops and turns 'round, "Yes?"

Wit' a tear or two formin', "I'm so tired... I'm just so tired, and I don't know wat' to do 'bout it."

She slowly walks to me to catch my tears in her hands as she palms my cheeks.

"It's okay to be tired, baby. God got greatness in ya', and He will give ya' rest. When he give ya' that time to let it out and be that light, be sho' to shine bright so we all can come a runnin' to ya' light."

She gives me a hug. That kinda hug where it even comfort my spirit and my body.

As she let's me go I tells her, "Goodnight Momma. I love ya."

I hear Momma walk back inside shuttin' the door behind her. I spring up to stand on the deck and look 'round the slave quarters one last time.

"I've been seein' a difference in you too!" From the shadows behind me, I hear a voice that makes me jump 'round real quick.

"Johnny! Wat' you doin' out?! And why ya' sneakin' up on somebody?" I says.

Steppin' on the porch from out the rain, Johnny- Boy walks up close to me. "I was up wit' Ado at the big house, workin'. Somethin' ya' uppity niggers ain't use to doin'."

I step in close to Johnny, "Hey, I told ya' 'bout that. It ain't right. Stop tellin' them lies. Don't be up there believin' everythin' that man tells you. He ain't doin' nothin' but-"

"But tellin' the truth!" Johnny Boy spurts out cuttin' me off.

"No! Not the truth. Lies. He ain't doin' nothin' but tryin' to gain favor wit' Massa' by puttin' us down 'cus he work up there instead of the fields like the dark skin folk."

"Folk? White people are folk. You and ya' kind are niggers. See that's wat' I mean, you been actin' real different lately, at least mo' then usual. Thinkin' ya' somethin' you ain't. You blame Ado and me for tryin' to be white, but we know our place. You tryin' get mo'. Mo' than wat' you should and be somethin' you ain't. Why is that Reagor? Wat' you been up to?"

"I ain't got time for ya', Johnny. Bye!" I turn to head inside the shack house. Johnny jumps in front of me.

"Why you so scared to say? Ado told me 'bout ya'... he told me wat's been happenin'. You know wat' I think, I think you been off wit' them other niggers tryin' to runaway. You tired all the time. Always stayin' up late. Is that it? You wanna runaway boy?" Johnny spews his venom at me, piercin' hard into my eyes. I can tell he tryin' to get a rise out of me. *Lord, don't let me give him one.*

Johnny steps closer to me and talk loud enough fo' only us two to hear,

"Best believe, if I find out somethin' I might have to share wit' fa—, Massa' Mills, wat' you been up to."

Wit' all my strength, I quickly grabs Johnny up by the collar and spin him 'round to hang him over the edge of the porch and begin to shows him a little bit of the new Reagor,

"First off, I'm the big brotha'. I tell you wat' you can do. 'Round here, I let ya' know wat' will happen. Now, I haven't been doin' anythin', but if you and that high yellow nigger wanna run ya' mouth stirrin' up trouble go ahead. See how long you last."

"Don't ya' dare get in my face again 'less there is a white man 'round to save ya' from me. You hear me, boy!?"

No quicker after I says my piece, I shove him off the porch to land in the puddle of mud below.

I'm doin' wat' my father said. Be strong.

Sun. Aug 14, 1831: Three Month Evaluation

"Whatever they were, it makes no diff..."

"Diff-er-ence. It's like when things are not the same, like men and women, or chil'ren and adults. Get it?" Nat teaches me.

"...Difference to me. God shows personal favor... favoritism to no man-for those who seemed to be somethin' added nothin".

"Great, Reagor! You are gettin' better. Now wat' you think that means?" Nat asks me.

Smirkin' I give my answer, "That white people ain't made to be as special as they like to think they be."

Nat flashes a smile 'cross his face. "True. No person is better than another, and we shouldn't be made to feel or think like such."

"So then why we slaves? Why they tell us ova' and ova' again that they are? Why they kill us so? Even white Pastors got slaves to beat."

"I don't know it all, 'cus I ain't white to be able to tell ya.' But from wat' I see, they have to keep the lie goin' unless this whole thing comes crashin' down... my prayer is God uses us to bring it down."

Fo' the past months Nat has been sneakin' ova',havin' meetings, and showin' me how to read. I gotta' be honest, I've been confused 'bout how I feel. On one hand, durin' the workin' day, I can barely keep my mind on workin'. I long to learn wats' been keepin' it from me. My thoughts make me feel a belief that maybe I'm much mo' than this work. More than this hell I'm livin' in. Then I get filled wit' so much hate! Why do this to us? Why be willin' to kill us, use us, destroy us fo' the sake of them to live happy. Nat says they got willful ignorance, in that, they will is to look, feel, and stay ignorant to the evilness they soul is filled wit'.

On the other hand, I feel like soon this sneakin' 'round is gonna' catch up to us, and I fear wat' that means for me and my family. Not like we got enough to fight back. The white man got armies, weapons, and focus wit' 'em. Never to let a nigger slip outta' place one time for they can upset the way things are.

All the negro got is brokenness. Brokenness from the inside out. Part of me wishes I didn't come to know. If I just stayed a quiet slave that just worked, complained, and waited for death to come hit me up 'cross the head, maybe things would be mo' simple. Ya' know, learn to enjoy the shackles on my mind and body.

"Nat, who taught ya' how to read?" I asked.

"When I was a child, my old Massa' wife had seen fit to teach me some words. We use to sit down like this here and read the Bible. I believe God has made my mind different. I saw and knew stuff he was already teachin' me just from hearin' stuff 'round the plantation. He was a nice Massa' to me. Barely hit me or yelled at me, but he taught me how to read for his purposes. She taught me how me bein' a nigger was God's way of given us purpose on this here earth and 'dat we needed white folk to gain back our favor wit' God when we die. Her husband would call me her special nigger."

"Her husband be evil to the slave women. He liked to beat 'em, brand 'em, and rape 'em. At night you always hear a woman screamin' for mercy at Massa's house followed by a laugh of enjoyment. He would call them the 'beasts of the night he had to conquer.' He even let the Overseers take our women for a night. Ones he didn't want no mo'."

"Yeah... I know 'bout that too, I've seen that done to my Momma." I says. "I was young watchin' in the corner but wasn't strong enough to help my Momma."

"I feel bad for all the lies I taught negroes. When I came to see the light and the truth, I promised to be different. If God is real and 'dis here book is true, He got to let me make it right and free our people."

Wit' a stillness in the air, I muster up the strength to ask this gut wrenchin' question to Nat. "Do you believe we was made black and they white fo' a purpose?"

Nat lookin' at the floor as his face reacts wit' a smirk, he raises his head, "I don't know... but wat' I have learned is that bein' born a negro is not a reason to be placed in bondage, shackled 'round constant hate. Just as bein' born white doesn't make ya' pure, right, and born above righteousness."

"I've wished to be white for so long. I thought that maybe if I was white, maybe I could have done somethin' fo' my dad. So many nights I stared at my battered blackened hands and just prayed for the chance to pull this wretched skin off hopin' maybe there be a feelin' that would come ova' me. A feelin' of... I don't know..."

"... a feelin' of wat' livin' is." Nat pieces the right words to my feelings.

I nod agreein'.

I start to ask Nat, "How we protect wat' is found disgustin'? How I care fo' my color if everythin' 'round me says it should be left for dead? I hate it... I hate them."

"True justice doesn't favor. True justice lifts the right and punishes the wrong. I've grown in lovin' myself, and we all must do so. For so much we have been told is wrong. If it takes death, we shall protect our people. In protectin' and freein' our people, we must not take up the very weapons used against us as I foresee them comin' back to harm us."

After pausin' Nat keeps on, "Our differences should not be feared, but serve a collective purpose yet, we are all too blinded to see. First we must remove our blindfolds and then we will seek the Lord on wat's next. Hate 'em if you want Reagor, white peoples' actions has made hate a reasonable response. Will ya' hate bring ya' peace? Unity within and outside? My biggest fear was allowin' my hate to make me the same as them."

"Dat's a lot of thinkin' to do. Dat' could be dangerous." Is the only thing I could come up wit' lookin' at all Nat placed at my feet.

For the first time I saw Nat do somethin' strange. He smiled wit' joy and said, "True, but I'mma a dangerous man. You will be too."

As we use 'dis stolen time to enjoy each other our 'tention is captured. Behind us we hear shufflin' in the distance. Nat looks over his shoulder and slowly bends down to pick up a stick. Then we listen to the call,

"Chirp -Chirp.... Chirp -Chirp... Chirp-Chirp,"

Comin' through the blankets be Jack, Will, Henry, Hark, and Nelson.

"Safe passage?" Nat asks.

"Safe passage. How ya'll be?" Hark says.

"Well, we be well. Shall we get started?" Nat asks while we all come together in a circle.

After a few moments, I ask Will, "Sam not comin'?"

Will sadly says, "No, he ain't comin' tonight."

"What happened?" Nat asks worried.

"He.... he stayed back to tend to his wife. They got whipped for stealin' some bread."

"Ain't... Ain't she wit' child?" Hark cuts in.

Will is shakin' his head as he gathers his words.

"Yeah. She took some pieces of bread while cleanin' in the house. His Massa' found it in her apron. He had Sam dig a hole deep and wide enough fo' her to put her belly inside so he can give her lashes. Sam then had to take five lashes' cus he stayed and helped her instead of finishin' his work."

We takes a moment of silence for our brotha.

"Dis here is the last meetin' men. Soon and very soon, the Lord will deliver the vision on how and when to move. How goes the word?" Nat asks.

"We have done wat' Reagor said. We 'gon 'round talkin' to fellow negroes we trust. Some are wit' us, others are too scared to join us. Those scared though won't go runnin' off at the mouth."

"Okay. Henry and I have some men at the ready to fight at our plantation. So when it happens, it starts wit' us. Once we got the victory, we will bring wat' we got ova' to Nelson. Will, Sam, and Hark, y'all be the next places. Since y'all on small farms ova' there, it be easier and mo' quiet wit' the numbers we will have. Reagor, you be last 'fore we go out further."

All was agreed to.

"Now men, we can't forget why we doin' this." Nat encourages us, "Stay prayed up, stay strong, and true to the vision. We can get scared and back out. We can't let fear keep us in 'dis prison anymore. When we get chances to be better, to have more, we must believe and take those moments."

"I'll see 'bout deliverin' a message to Sam." Will says.

"Okay, thank you,"

"Safe passage home. Be blessed." Nat says.

As the rest start leavin', I bend ova' to pick up Nat's bag. It's the first time I got to touch it and it feels heavier than just one Bible.

"Here you go Nat," gettin' his attention.

He turns 'round and takes it from me, "Thank ya."

I get the courage to ask , "Wat' else is in there?"

"Keys to freedom."

"I hope you use 'em keys right," I says.

"Me too...me too. Before you go, think 'bout this Reagor 'till I see you again. Learn to do well. Seek judgment, relieve the oppressed; for it is written, Vengeance is mine; I will repay, saith the Lord."

"Safe Passage," I respond wit', listenin' to wat' he says to me.

Wit' a sigh of relief, I make it back to the shack safely. I open the door quietly, tryin' my damndest not to make a sound. I pick up my shirt-blanket and lean back into the chair. Hopefully, I can catch some sleep before the tower bell calls.

A few moments went by when I closed my eyes.

"Ahem, ahem."

"... ahem, ahem." 'Dat sound got louder.

"I peak my eyes open to find a pair of eyes starin' back at me from the floor. After a mouthful is exchanged by our eyes , Johnny- Boy turns ova' and lets out,

"Mmhm- mmhm..."

17

GOSSIP IN THE FIELDS - TUES. AUG 16, 1831

Tuesdays was Momma long days for work. She would start off her day workin' in the fields, but then by noontime, she'd go off to the side of the big house and help wit' laundry. I make it a point to get more than enough of my work done lil' bit faster on these days, so I can see to it to help her carry the clothes that need to be folded home.

I turn in my hoe and take for the day from the tobacco fields on my way back to the shacks. As I head up the hill, I see Momma and Ms. Cheryl talkin'. As I'm walkin' upwards, someone quickly jumps on my back,

"Hey, Reagor!" Sam says wit' excitement.

Strugglin' to hold his weight, I says, "Hey Sam, Boy! Get up off me now! You too heavy."

As quickly as I spoke the words, I lovingly toss him off me to get my breath,

"How was work?"

"Fine. The cane fields are a lil' easier than the cotton field to tend to. Afterwhile, ya' get used to swingin' that hatchet to cut it down and then just gotta' go back through and pick it up."

"Yeah, I know, cotton may be light, but it definitely ain't kind to ya' fingers pickin' it."

"Nathaniel did get some licks today for workin' slow, but I kept my head down and stayed workin' like you say," Sam responds.

I grab him up like only brothas do to show my joy of his actions while walkin' to Momma.

As we get closer to Momma and Ms. Cheryl, I can't help but wonder how 'dis new me would react to seein' a beatin'. Could I still watch? Would I offer help? Would I attack? Wat' would Nat say do?

Sam offers his greetings, "Hi Momma, Hi Ms. Cheryl."

"Hey boys, Eliza, these boys of yours just growin' like weeds! Glad to 'em always tendin' to they Momma."

"Yeah, Cheryl, sho' is a blessin'. Well, we gonna' get goin' to the house so I can get started on this foldin'."

Before walkin' away, I ask Ms. Cheryl, "You need me to carry that on down to ya' house?"

"No thank ya', I manage just fine. Thank ya'."

As she walks away, my eyes fixate on a small red flower she got on her dress.

"Hey Sam, go on and run these clothes down to the house for Momma," I says .

"Yes," he say as he grabs the bag wit' two hands.

As always, I help Momma on down the hill to get on home. By this time, everybody is makin' they way back from the fields. Momma is smilin' and wavin'. Usually, I'm focused on just gettin' to the house, but today somethin' else gets my attention. I count seven red flowers. As we walkin', we pass by Mr. Isaac, Mary Ann, Big John, Lil' Son, Scooter, and

Tommy. They all seem to be wearin' the same flower Ms. Cheryl have on. As we come to our humble shack, we see Johnny- Boy out on the porch eatin' some berries.

"Don't just look at me boy. Help ya' Momma up," Momma calls out to Johnny.

Johnny gets up to reach for her hand and pulls her up, "Yes, ma'am."

As she makes it up she gives him a kiss on the cheek, "thank ya' boy,"

He smiles in acceptance of his wages. Meanwhile, as I walk up and follow behind Momma in the house, Johnny greets me wit' a smirk as he stuffs his face wit' some mo' berries. After I come in, he follows me.

"Reagor, slide that table ova' and start pullin' them sheets out so I can get to foldin'."

"Yes Ma'am." I slide the bag ova' and pull the chair up in front of the table for Momma to sit at.

Sittin' on the bed, Johnny starts talkin' to Momma, "Hey Momma, guess wat' I heard today in the big house?"

"What you hear?"

"I heard some of the older slaves talkin' 'bout how there's been talk of fightin' the Massa' and Overseers."

"Yeah, Ms. Cheryl was tellin' me 'bout that in the washroom today."

I keep my head down, tendin' to this here laundry. I notice Johnny's voice gettin' a lil' louder,

"Seems some niggers been sneakin' off in the woods or somewhere plottin',"

"Oh Lawd, have mercy,"

"Reagor, did ya' hear somethin' 'bout that?" Johnny-Boy asks puttin' his last berry in his mouth, smirkin'.

"I... I did hear somethin' like that, but I don't believe it, though."

"Really, why? I mean, it be so easy to run off wouldn't it. The woods is just right there..."

I look up, "I mean, hey, I think it's stupid. We all know the price of plottin' 'round here."

"Did anyone get caught doin' this?" Momma asks.

"Naw, not yet, but if they do, ya' know it's gonna' be high time for some hangings." Johnny-Boy replies.

Momma interjects, "Johnny! Don't be talkin' like that in this house."

"Wat' Momma? I'm just speakin' the truth. I mean the nigger that want to mess up this here good livin' should be punished."

"Don't you mean negroes? I think you said mo' than one, right?!" I looks at him right angry.

"And wat' good livin' you talkin' 'bout boy?" I spew at Johnny- Boy.

"Some good livin', we ain't got enough food to feed all of us. Oh, maybe you mean the good livin' of havin' one bed for four people? Maybe the good livin' is doin' nothin'... nothin' but WORKIN'' TO DEATH!" I shout throwin' the rest of the sheets on the table.

I intensely stare at Johnny seein' past his brown eyes to see his blackened evil spirit findin' joy in gettin' me upset.

Lookin' at me dead in the eye, wit' a big smile, Johnny-Boy utters, "You be an ungrateful nigger."

Unable to keep myself, I run ova' and jump on top of Johnny-Boy on the bed wit' my hands tight 'round his neck.

"I told you, don't be callin' me no nigger! I ain't ya' nigger!"

Momma start hittin' my back. "Get off him, Reagor! Get up off him now!" Momma shouts.

Too angry to see anything but Johnny's scrawny neck in my swole stiff hands, I hear Johnny say, "Keep it up, and I'll let Massa' who's doin' wat'.... Boy..."

"SLAP!"

Was the sound that came when Momma's hand met wit' my face, "I said, get off him, Reagor!"

As I slowly get off and let Johnny- Boy go, I storm outside, slammin' the door behind me.

If God was to ever show, I need him to hurry up and let it be known.

Mon. Jan 7, 1811: Charles Deslondes Manifesto

Down in New Orleans, slaves is known for growin' up the sweetest sugar cane in all of America.

Guess we able to make it so sweet 'cus everythin' else 'round us ain't sweet. In fact, everythin' else 'round us is anything but sweet. God as my witness tho' tonight will be the last night, for we take to the streets tomorrow shoutin', "Freedom or Death!".

All 'dis week I layed up every nite thinkin' why the Lord placed this burden on me to lead these slaves? Why curse me wit' the tainted mind of desirin' freedom? Why stir up trouble knowin' that if we get caught, I'd be responsible for spreadin' this mindset 'round that brought death to all these others slaves willin' to follow me? Why fight for somethin' you ain't never had?

My momma told me that my very life is livin' proof that a slave's life and body isn't theirs. My father and Massa', Manuel Andry, took my momma in the night. It was known to be the best way to produce labor wit'out cost.

The Lord saw fit to brand me light skin and skilled. Massa' Andry saw fit to burden me wit' the role as his driver when I came of age, the highest rank for a nigger in his domain.

For wat' may have looked like a good thing wasn't. Massa' Andry gave me a title and role that could make one feel as if they was more than a nigger. To all the whites 'round my role and color said, 'this one can be trusted a bit'. To other slaves, it said, 'this one can't be trusted.' Disowned from my own. Perhaps Massa' Andry thought he was showin' tenderness towards me due to me bein' his son, yet in grantin' me a certain level of favor, he just gave me different shackles. Ones wrapped around the heart and mind.

I was given the additional duties of makin' sure the slaves got up in the mornin' and watch ova' the slaves from day-to-day. Report wat' was known and wat' I had seen. Massa' Andry's biggest command was to be responsible for buck breakin' new slaves upon arrival. My people. As he said, "I want the whippins' so hard that it drives the lazy far away from them. Can't have savage beasts not bein' wat' they were bred to be." His heart birthed no tolerance for wat' he thought nothin' of.

After each public whippin' or breakin' was ova', Massa' Andry would ask me in front of all in attendance, "Does it weigh heavy on ya' heart to inflict this pain on ya' own kind?"

Knowin' the answer required of me from previous lessons, I would respond, "No, sir. I feel nothin' of the sort."

Yet no one knew my true heart in that it was far too hard to bear more pain than that which already existed. For every lashin' I gave out, that lashin' came 'cross my own soul. Those that saw me do it may have thought I took joy in it, but far from it. It was forgotten we all have been put in a system that destroys us all.

This power based on bein' obsessed wit' given' off evil dominance... based on forcin' people to fall underneath the strength of the whip and fear, yet us that are under it know it's not true power. It's witchcraft meant to bend and twist a man's will against himself for the gain of yourself. It's a prison for the inflicted and the inflictor, for no matter how tender my father was toward me, it could never rival the cemented boundaries of color. For rankin' and position must be followed 'til death for the system to remain and its effect intact.

I could no longer bear this role anymore...

The isolation of my position, yet not wanted from either side... set alone, forgotten to die alone. No more! I choose! I choose to gain the honor and respect of my own! I choose to stand or fall alongside righteousness and combat the false power. Wit' the good sense God gave me, I seized this chance that has put me on the path of rebellion.

Massa' Andry gave me permission to go to other plantations 'round us and to town for his biddin'. I used this permission to set forth a plan in motion. Wit' takin' advantage of my role for the good of my people, that's how I gained my people's respect and trust. This is how I got them to believe wit' action on one accord. Despite the forced divide, I would not let it stay between us, for we are all endurin' suffrage we must come together to get out of. That is why the 500 of us are ready to face the bloodshed tomorrow brings.

In watchin' the white folks, I've learned the wisdom of thinkin', leadership, and unity for a common goal in military efforts. I've seen their belief that niggers are without a mind provide niggers a secret strength. We are good at hidin' it but must use it when time is right. For even in our plan, we will hide our flesh wit' the clothes of soldiers.

The other slave leaders and I have decided the best day will be tomorrow for the start of the Carnival celebration, and the continued war wit' the Spanish gives us the best chance to rise up as one. Many of the dragoons have been called away. Wit' our 500, we will storm the weapon house! This is our time to see them as we see ourselves! They are mere men wit' no hold over our lives for we will take our freedom!

I've come to gain the trust in my people for wat' I showed them I am before I told them. Andry made them fear me because of how he used me. I wanted to prove I'm not that for which I was used for, but I am what I make of myself to be. I was made to bring us together for a goal that was worth fightin' for.

I pen these thoughts wit' all my heart, for I want this moment to live past me, past us. I don't know if we shall live past tomorrow, but I know that we took a stand for wat' is right. In tryin' to separate us, we can come together as one. The strength of slavery is rooted in daily violence, continued lies, and creating levels of division inside a person and the people. Our strength is in sheddin' of fear, becomin' one, willin' to believe in wat' is ours.

If we don't make it, I pray that these words find one to use them wisely.

It is better to die for justice and bravery than to be shackled to silence and evil.

After readin' the words left behind, Nat places the papers back into the bag and hides them for the last time under the floorboards. He gets on his knees to pray fo' strength and help for wat' comes next.

Sat. Aug. 20, 1831 11:00PM: Cabin Pond

"Nat, you sho' you don't want none of this here swine?" Hark asks for the fifth time.

"Yes, sir. I'm sure. Y'all go 'head and enjoy."

"I ain't steal this pig and good brandy for nothin' now. Shoot, this might be the last time ever we eat on this here side of life. Might as well go out wit' some good food in ya' stomach.

"Yes, I'm sure."

"Where's that boy Reagor? He looks like he needs a meal or two. He comin'?" Hark asks.

"No I didn't tell him about this meetin'. It's just for us here. We are the ones that started this, we will be the first so it's important for us to be on one accord."

"I like 'em! He quiet, and stays out the way." Nelson says.

"He's too quiet, can we trust him? How you know he ain't goin' back tellin' and settin' us up?" Jack proposes.

Hark quickly swallowin' his bite of food shares his thoughts, "Well, he ain't done nothin' yet but wat we ask. So I think we can trust him, plus he been teachin' me how to count. I like 'em."

Nelson comments, "Plus he got more balls then any of us at his age. At that age, I did any and everythin' my Massa' wanted no questions. I found my happiness bein' up under Massa."

"That's cus' you a house negro. He be like me, out in 'dem fields workin'. It's easy to not like ya' own for you see yaself. And any bit of information to get some food, or day off.... I've seen negroes tell on others for less." Jack says.

"He's got somethin' great in 'em. He can be trusted and if he follows the right path he may become the best of us all. Now, before this whole time get 'way from us. I want to make sho' we set for tomorrow. Will, was you able to get the word out?" Nat asks.

"Yes, sir," he says, showin' off his small red flower. "Everyone has been wearin' them all week to get the word out so everybody can see." Will answers.

"Good, good. Henry, Nelson, Hark, how we lookin' on weapons?"

"We got them all sharp and ready to go. Even wit' workin' in the mornin' the tools be good for fightin'."

133

"Good, good. Men. 'Dis time tomorrow will be the fight for it all. We have sought after the kingdom, and that time has arrived. We have prepared, and we plotted well. We have waited on the hand of the Lord, and He shall be wit' us. God is no respecter of persons, and bondage is meant for no man. We was torn away and brought here; place that on ya' hearts. Think 'bout all we have seen, all the pain we have witnessed, all the hardships endured up 'til now. Just like America fought for their freedom and fought for wat' they believed was right, we will do the same.

Jerusalem is where we are headed, men! We will take it as our promise-land. I'll see to it.

<u>SECTION 3</u>

18

THE DIVINE RED SIGN - SUN. AUG 21, 1831

"Bong! Bong!"
"Bong! Bong!"

The tower bell rings. It felt like only a short whil' ago I fell asleep, and it's already time for work.

As I fought a losin' fight to get up, I said to myself, *need to start sleepin'.*

As I slowly rose to my feet, I looked out the window and saw that it was still dark as night outside.

"Bong! Bong!"
"Bong! Bong!"

"Reagor, baby, is it time to get up?" Momma says soft in my ear bein' woke up to the tower bell.

I respond, "I'm not sure, Momma. It's still pitch black out there. Let me go take a look."

I throws on my blanket shirt for some warmth as I step outside on the porch. I look up to the sky and see the sun ain't nowhere to be seen. I don't know if Massa' is losin' it or wat'.

"Hey, Reagor! Wat' that is?!" Shouts Johnson from cabin four.

"I'm not sure! I'mma go up and check,"

"Okay, let me know if it is time to go. The sun ain't comin' up fo' a whil'." He yells back.

I jump down off the porch and walk on up to my hill to see the big house closer without bein' seen.

Somethin' unusual was goin' on up there. I point my ear towards the house to hear betta'. It sounded to me like some fightin' goin' on ... and wrestlin' of stuff bein' broken. I look back up at the house and see some torches lit up all 'round the house. As dark as it was, it look like light bugs flickerin' in the night sky. As I turn back, the bell rings off again.

"Bong! Bong!"

By now, all us have heard the bell ring couple a' times, so I jump up the porch and walk back into the shack. I take a minute to think 'bout how none of this is right, 'specially how often the bell has rung. Ado usually only gives us two rings. After that, the Overseers start marchin' on down here to start whippin' folks to work.

"Well, Reagor, wat's happenin'?" Sam asks, sittin' up on the bed.

"I'm not sho,' but I think it's best we go ahead and make our way up there to go find out together," I says calmly to keep spirits still.

"Sam, you take Johnny- Boy and go ahead and knock 'round to get people up. I'mma help Momma, it's pretty dark out there, okay?" I request.

"Yes, sir," Sam answers.

"And y'all stay together, alright? Don't go too far."

"Yes, sir," Sam says as he is pullin' Johnny- Boy out the door who's still tryin' wake up.

I help Momma quickly get her stuff together so we can go 'head and make this walk.

As we walk, my mind is racin'. It's goin' through different thoughts as to wat' is happenin'. Maybe Massa' is tryin' to see who is here and who ain't... did Johnny say somethin'? Did someone else say somethin'? Wat' if they ask me somethin'?

Wit' every step Momma and I make towards the house, wit' every passin' ring, my heart races a lil' faster. I don't care much for this feelin'.

"Baby, who them negroes holdin' them torches?" Momma asks.

I respond, "I'm... I'm not sho' Momma." They clearly ain't from here. Certainly ain't dressed like slaves. As I look 'round, I see... I see blood on the ground... it's all ova'.

As everyone from the shacks stand 'round, we start lookin' 'round for some answers as to wat' we have woke up to. I take a breath, I start lookin' at the faces of the men and women holdin' torches. I notice the blood red stains on their faces and clothes shimmerin' in the fiery light.

I look to the back and I sees Nelson and Will are tuggin' hard at the rope. They the ones that sounded the tower bell. Watchin' 'em, you hear 'em gruntin' loud as they pull together. You hear the splitting of the wood on the staircase where the bell tower is. Soon after, the large brass bell comes crashin' down hard to the ground destroyin' the Massa's well-kept flowers! Nelson and Will celebrate their hard efforts. I look 'round at the faces 'round me all showin' worry, fear, or not understandin'.

Out of the crowd, a voice shouts, "Look up! Is that Massa'?"

Out of the darkness at the top of the staircases emerges Nat lookin' 'round at the conquered spoils.

The fight has begun!

There's a death like silence holdin' the tongue of all the slaves. Wat' captures my sight is the look of Nat and his command right now. As he is comin' down the stairs you can see he's dressed in a fine sharp white buttoned shirt wit' bloodstains 'cross the front fittin' for only a white man to wear. He is wearin' a matchin' pattern outfit, 'though his black pants are a little short as it don't go all the way down to cover his ankles. You can tell he been on his knees wit' the mud and grass stains as a giveaway. His black jacket and vest have no holes. The jacket and vest have no worn look to it.

He has shed the shackles and clothes of a slave and is wearin' the clothes of a man.

Nat makes his way to the stage and waves us to come in closer. As he is pacin' back and forth waitin' for us to come, I can see his hatchet attached to his hand. The worn wooden handle has deep ridges on it wit' curves. The base look to be wrapped in burlap fo' grip. Once he stands, you can see the thick head of the hatchet still drippin' fresh blood. Nat wipes the blood splats ova' his face before he start talkin',

"Fellow negroes! Calm yaselves and heed my words. Nat Turner, my men, and I have come to set you free. First, I must apologize to ya'. Apologize for the lies that I was forced to say, apologize for the harm my words of the false gospel have brought upon ya' in makin' you believe the good Lord wanted you to remain slaves for ya' earthly life. I was also a slave and served a Massa' that used me for my gifts, talents, and skill. My work was to make you work harder, enjoy your suffrage, and never question your place in life. In my journey for God, He revealed himself to me and showed me the devil has infiltrated this land and is usin' the white folks to do the work of death towards us. For years, our people have bled, died, cried, and prayed fo' deliverance. Well, God has 'quipped us to be that answer to those prayers!"

The rustlin' of us slaves show we still tryin' to understand.

For the first time, the death 'round us aint comin' for us, but for the whites. I turn to look at Momma, Sam, and Johnny. Momma is clutchin' onto Sam tight in a way I remember whil' Johnny has an angry look. Most times, it's the one he gives to me when he don't like my words. As the chatter amongst the slaves grow, a voice shouts out,

"Wat' now!? You know they goin' to come to kill us all now!? Wat' we to do?!"

"I see and know that not tellin' all of ya' of our plans we have taken away ya' choice to decide. I thought it better to take ya' choice and give you freedom since thus far, our choice was taken and only given bondage! We are headed to free more. We will grow and seek God's call as to how to obtain freedom for our people. The adversary will fight us and will fight this change, but we will win! Those who want to join and fight step forward! Leave behind the shackles and loyalty to ya' Massa' who only wants you to profit him! Join us!"

"And where is my Massa' boy?!" Ado, drunk wit' rage, jumps in front of the stage.

"Wat' makes you think we don't like this here?! We got a good thing goin', and you uppity niggers believe you can just come up 'round here killin' off white folks?! No sir! I won't go wit' you. Now, where is my Massa?!... Did you kill him boy?"

Standin' by, I see Nat swirlin' and grippin' his hatchet wit' his right hand as he stares at Ado. Controlin' his breathin' and emotion, Nat slowly walks to the edge of the stage and bends down low to meet Ado's face.

"First, I'mma man. Don't ever make that mistake again. Second, if you want ya' Massa' I'll get him for ya'."

Nat rises to his feet, never breakin' his eyes off Ado, who is backin' into a defeated pose.

"Henry! Hark! Bring 'em out!" Nat shouts backin' up towards the big house.

We all look to the house as we see Henry and Hark draggin' Massa' Mills out of his house bound in rope and gagged. Not carin' theys drag Massa' Mills up on the stage as if... as if he was a negro. Even wit' his tusslin' and fightin', he went up on that stage. Hark makes him slide to the edge of the stage on his knees, forced to look at all us negroes.

I couldn't make out Massa' Mills at first. He didn't have his joy. He didn't have his strength. The blood pourin' from his mouth and stomach may have had somethin' to do wit' it. Wat' was most enjoyable was seein' the defeated look in his weepin' eyes. The helplessness of his body. Even when Ado tried to rush the stage to offer him aid, Hark and Henry shout at him,

"Get back! Get back! Don't touch him!"

I'm sure the rifles they had hangin' ova' they shoulders is why Ado took orders from some negroes. Nat walks behind Massa' Mills and harshly rubs his shoulders and face continuously and says,

"The mere fact I am touchin' him, I could be killed by his standards. I'm sure his soul is cryin' for help thinkin' that somehow by a touch, he is given some type of leprosy that can only be removed by killin' me."

Massa' Mills steady tried to get this feelin' to stop, but Nat stopped when he wanted to.

Nat slings him to the floor and says, "How many times has he and his men touched you? Killed ya' sons, mommas, or daddies? How many times has he laid hands on your wives? Forced himself upon them without so much as a thought? Harmed the women for his sinful needs while sayin' they are the problem for his lack of control. How many has he lynched on these here ropes for ya'll to see?"

Mrs. Cheryl steps out. Nat stands to his feet. She begin to walk and stand wit' the others that came wit' Nat. Followin' her lead, Mr. Isaac, Mary Ann, Big John, Lil' Son, Scooter, and Tommy, walk ova'. Massa' Mills staggers to sit back upright.

Nat keeps on, "How many times has he stripped your manhood, taken your kids, dismembered ya' body for the purpose of structure, fun, and way of life. If death is assured by stayin' and ya' won't ever be seen as a human in their sight, take the opportunity to fight wit' us in gettin' our humanity back!"

Nat was steady clinchin' his hatchet tighter and tighter. Like a good preacher on Sunday mornin', his emotion could no longer be caged. He stands on the edge of the stage next to Massa' Mills,

"Far too much bloodshed has been spilled in this country!"

"... to not be answered by blood!"

Wit' one swift strike Nat's hatchet creates a moment where all hearts are clinched wit' shock and relief. In this moment, we hearin' a red waterfall givin' a answer. In this moment, all eyes are not believin'. Massa' Mills head has fallin' away from his body onto the ground in front of us. Nat kicks his body off the stage to be wit' the rest.

19

Shift in the Atmosphere - Sun. Aug 21, 1831

"No!! Boy wat' have you done!?" Ado cryin' ova' the lifeless remains of Massa' Mills. Other slaves rush to carefully grab his head and begin to weep ova' his body. His hold on the loyalty of these slaves can't be stopped by even death. Even wit' all he done to us... even wit' all he done to me and my family... I couldn't explain the tears I shed for him standin' there.

Johnny-Boy was the only one of us to be joinin' in on protectin' Massa's body. A cluster of slaves ran off and anotha' cluster was stiff wit' fear. The rest us carefully back away to put space 'tween us and wat' was happenin'. Nat walks down off the stage from the left side, grabbin' a torch from one of his soldiers.

As he grabs the torch he sends out a order, "Ready the men and horses."

Nat walks five paces closer to us. "Brothas' and Sistas' calm yaselves. I know 'dis here alot to take in, but in time... this moment, we must walk in faith and move wit' action for our divine purpose! Tonight we leave victimhood and all it's shackles on the ground. We bear our wounds and scars proudly to strengthen us in movin' forward. Please, don't be comfortable in ya' shackles that you have let your hope for better die. Comfort is death. Wit' seekin' true justice it won't be given. The last thing I will do is force any negro, man or woman, to follow for my purpose."

From the shadows all 'round we see at least fifty men and women come up by foot, or by horse, or ridin' in a wagon filled wit' money, food, tools, and weapons. They also brought ova' Massa' Mills five horses and Ado's drivin' wagon.

Walkin' behind Nat a man hands him the reins of a horse, Nat turns to climb aboard, "The choice is yours. Wat' say you this evenin'?"

Slowly, men and women make a choice. So far only eleven walks to join. Nat and I lock eyes.

"... And wat' say you?"

I slowly walk forward. I turn 'round and face Momma still holdin' onto Sam's hand capturin' this still image for my memory. I walk toward 'em to hug 'em both for as hard and as long as we could bear.

"Momma, I'mma go wit' them. I must do this...." I stand tall announcin' as tears race down my face.

"You wat'?! You ain't goin' nowhere! We have to... we must stay together!"

"Momma, I've been workin' wit' them for the longest on this here revolt." Lettin' them know wat' I been up to.

Momma's arms fall off of Sam to cover her mouth. Sam stands tall wit' those big brown eyes tryin' to hold back his sadness.

"Reagor, baby, why did you do this? Why... why would you bring this death here? I needs to understand!" she shouts at me while grabbin' me to catch herself from fallin' to the floor. 'Stead she falls into my chest and begins to sob. I hold her close for I know, and she know this may be the last time we get to hug.

I pull her back and look her in the eyes, "Momma you have been everythin' I've needed. You've kept us together and have never complained. I learned so much from you. Wat' you mean to me words can't say, but Momma you deserve so much better than death. You deserve much mo' than a life in chains and fear... we all do! I believe it so much I'm willin' to go get it for us. Whatever it cost, it sho' 'nuff worth it. I must go off and be wat' I'm meant to be. I'm not sho' wat' that is yet, but I know somethin' within me is sayin' this is my way to go."

I hold Momma close again.

As we hug I look ova' at Sam and we lock tear filled eyes. I pull him in close to join in this family moment.

I say in his ear, "Sam, I love you brotha! Stay safe, stay close wit' Momma, and wat' else?"

As he pulls away to look at me, he wipes his face and answers wit', "Be strong,"

Momma pulls away, and wit' a hurtin' voice she finds the strength to say, "Reagor, Son, I love you dearly! You stepped into ya' role in this family and ya' Dad will be proud in that you've done wat' he always told ya' to... be strong."

Momma grabs my face wit' a grip of love and kisses my face. She wipes away my tears and says, "I know God has a plan for you! We gonna' be alright!"

I find the strength to back away slow from 'em.

As I turn to walk to Nat, Johnny-Boy is still hunched ova' wit' the rest ova' Massa' Mills body. I walk to him and place my head on his shoulder to turn him,

"Johnny—"

"POW!"

Johnny's fist came 'cross my face knockin' me back a few only to be tackled by him,

"I hate you! I hate you! Ya' dirty nigger! I hope you die... you let this happen! You let this happen to mine just like you let it happen to yours!"

Nelson rushes ova' to throw Johnny off me and help me to my feet. Johnny tries to come back but Nelson raises his hatchet to keep him at a distance sayin',

"Alright boy! Stay back now."

"Reagor, you knew this was comin' and you did nothin' to stop it and save our family!" wit' tears and anger spillin' out all ova' Johnny keeps on, "All the sneakin' out, all the fights wit' me. I knew I should have said somethin'! You a dead nigger walkin'! All of ya'!"

All I could do was stand. In spite of how hard his words were, I stood tall. Wit' Johnny and I standin' 'cross from one anotha' I felt somethin'. Somethin' new that I haven't in all my life.

Pity.

In all that I done for him. Loved him, took to him, never makin' him feel less than...

I give in and look at 'em. I walk ova' to climb aboard the horse wit' Nat, bein' a witness to all this unfold, then I stop.

I walk ova' and snatch a torch from the woman standin' by the wagon and run ova' to get on top of the stage.

"Massa' Mills is no longer my Massa' no more!" I shout to those that are still 'round as I point the torch ova' his dismembered body wit' my so called brotha' lookin' up at me. I shout out, "I burn the ropes that he used to take my father away!" as I set them ablaze.

"I burn this tree that has been used as a tool to cause so much death!" As I set the torch next to the tree the fire quickly runs through the dried out tree trunk spreadin' from top to bottom. As the tree goes up in flames, the crowd shouts in celebration. I step back and 'fore I drop the torch on the stage floor I shout, "'Dis here is fo' my real brotha who faced evil wit' no fear! Fo' I will follow his lead to be strong!"

I jump off stage and step back 'round to bask in the warmth and the energy from the fire and crowd for a spell. As the cheers go up while watchin' the fire grow and not willin' to be tamed, that's wat' was happenin' in our spirits as we marched out wit' a purpose. Freedom is wat' we strivin' to have in this land and we are goin' to see it come to past.

I come back 'round and mount back up on the horse wit' Nat and the slavery army scatterin'. I wave bye to Momma and Sam. I pray a silent prayer, "Lawd, if you are out there, keep them."

Lookin' back I see Johnny standin' in front of the fire watchin' all us ride off.

Just as the last of us pull away, Johnny starts runnin' the other way. One thing 'bout Johnny, he too will strive for wat' he wants, 'specially when he done feel he got wronged.

Sun. Aug 21, 1831 11:15 PM: Preparation

Nat's heavenly ordered steps are pointin' us to Jerusalem. Jerusalem is where we meant to be settin' up God's mission, accordin' to Nat. In order to get there, mo' plantations gotta' be overtaken, many mo' slaves need to be freed and fight, and some whites have to die.

He broke me from my shackles, so who am I to say wat's leadin' him as long as I gets justice and my freedom. We head for the plantations of

Dr. Blunt, Mr. Salathiel and Nathaniel Francis, Captain Barrow, Ms. Vaughan, and Mr. James Parker.

Based on the word from Jack, Will, and Nelson, Mr. Nathaniel Francis has the strongest black bucks in all of Southampton County since they always have the best crop yields 'round. Dr. Blunt's plantation is farther up towards the tip of the county. He is the doctor who tends to white folks 'round here, and if need be, he will look at slaves. Perhaps they gots too harsh a whippin' but they Massa' needed him or her to live. Dr. Blunt be the one they call. At times he brought wit' him some female slaves who would assist him in lookin' since he won't dare touch a nigger himself.

"Okay men! We just 'bout a mile from Mr. Nathaniel Francis' plantation. Take a minute to get ya' mind right for we gon' ride off from here." Nat tells us. Whil' the insurrection brigade catch their breath, Nat gathers the leaders together for orders.

"Henry, Sam, and Nelson, I want you to take twenty people wit' ya'. Use the cover of the night to help get you up to Dr. Blunt's Farm. That's 'bout an eighteen-mile journey. You should make it 'fore daybreak. Be quick to take the land, collect those willin' to come, collect wat' you can take then be on ya' way. I'mma take Will, Hark, Reagor, and fifteen men wit' me up towards Francis Farm. After victory, we gon' move ova' to Captain Barrow Farm. Meet us at high noon on the east side of the woods, 'bout a mile outside Vaughan's plantation in a day's time. Jack, you are in charge here. Stay wit' the rest here, 'til we come get ya' to go 'on to Barrow's Farm."

All was in agreement. Nelson, Henry, and Sam go to the wagon wit' the weapons and collects a hatchet, ax, and riffle for themselves. They takes a look at the brigade and choose twenty to grab a weapon. Once they come together, they march into the woods. 'Dis is a moment Momma would say a prayer fo' they safety.

As they become one wit' the night, I walk up to the weapon wagon to look inside. Who knew wit' all these tools I held in my hand every day, I could have been usin' 'em to get somethin' I never knew I wanted.

Liberty.

"Hand me that there musket, boy," Henry asks of me from behind.

I turn to look at him, then I quickly pull out the closest one and hand it to him. "Here ya' go."

"Thank ya'. You ready?" Henry asks.

"To go? Ya' let's go." I answer thinkin' we 'bout to walk away. He puts his hand into my chest to stop me. I look back up at him.

"No, I mean you ready for wat's to come?" Henry asks.

"Wat's to come?"

"We 'bout to take somethin' we ain't neva' had. We have done and believed stuff that's a white man's worst nightmare. Wat's 'bout to come is a meeting of both sides misunderstandin'. A misunderstandin' of who we think we are against wat' they think we should be. We gotta' go let them know how serious we be. How serious are you, Reagor?"

After a pause, I says, "Very?"

Henry's eyes have a look so bright it makes the night scared to come 'round his face. He shook his head and said, "Not good 'nough. I need you to get like me... get dead serious."

Nat waves for me to join his fifteen chosen men.

We ride to Francis Plantation.

20

THE INSURRECTION - MON. AUG 22, 1831

Aug 22, 1831 12:30 AM: Insurrection: Salathiel Francis Plantation

Crouched in the woods, we see a clear view of the Overseer Cabin and Francis' house.

"So how we gonna' do this?" Will asks.

"Dis here wat' we do. R eagor and I gon' walk up to the door. We gonna' say we got a message for Massa' Francis. You gonna' take this gun and stand on one side of the window. ark, you take the other gun and you be on the other window. You each take two men wit' ya' for numbers. On my signal, we gonna' attack and you gonna' shoot them from the window. Okay?" Nat instructs.

"Wat' 'bout the rest of us?"

Nat turns 'round to look at all the eager and scared faces hangin' on his word, "Once you hear the gunshots y'all stand tall wit' y'all weapons and run towards Francis house and break the front door down. Be sho' to cover the back of the house and the front. Kill any man, woman, child dat's white inside. Once we done wit' the Overseers, we comin' ova' to help."

"Follow me," Nat says to me. We make our way to the front of the Overseer's cabin door. Nat takes a deep breath and mumbles a word to himself. He stretches out his left hand to knock wit' his right behind his back, wit' his hatchet firm in his hand.

"KNOCK, KNOCK"
"KNOCK, KNOCK"

Nat puts both hands behind his back, head bowed down low. Lookin' at him, I follow his lead and do the same. We hear steps comin' toward the door, and someone undoes the lock. The door cracks open just 'nough for the Overseer to shine a lamp out to see who's at the door.

He shouts at us,

"Boy! Who you?! Wat' you doin' out here this late?!"

Nat answers while takin' a piece of paper out his left pocket. He holds it up wit' his left hand, "Sorry Sir, Massa' Mills sent us up here wit' an urgent message for Massa' Francis."

"Ugh, wakin' me up like this here! I got a good mind to take my belt..." The Overseers says outloud. We hear 'em say it through the closed door and hear him undue the other lock. He swings the door open wide 'nough to see three other white men inside wit' him—one by each window in they beds and one layin' in the top bed.

"Well, gon' give it to me, boy!" He angrily spews at Nat.

I keep my head low thinkin' if he sees my eyes, I'd give away somethin'.

Nat slowly hands ova' the folded piece of paper to the man.

As he started unfoldin' the blank paper, Nat shouts out,

"NOW!"

"SPLAAT!" "SPLAAT!"

Wit' the speed of a dartin' rabbit, Nat brings 'round his hatchet and lands it right into the neck of the Overseer. He quickly pulls it back and hits him one more time. As I look up, his blood comes rainin' 'cross my face. Nat shoves the bleedin' white man down to the floor.

The white men layin' in bed had only 'nough time to witness their friend's death before they too were met wit' hot lead comin' from the windows. Nat walks quickly inside and bury the hatchet wit' all the men just to make sure no one was left alive.

I'm frozen at the front door like my legs are stuck in mud. The only thing I can move are my eyes. I'm no stranger to death. I've seen whippins' so bad it tore the skin clear off some slaves' back.

Witnessin' niggers not on the receivin' end of death... Seein' pure white blood bein' spilled and splattered underneath the feet of a negro... It's new.

"Reagor! Reagor!" Nat shouts at me while shakin' me.

I take my focus off the pools of blood and bodies to look at him, "Yes? Yes?"

"Come 'on, we got to go join the rest!" Nat shouts before takin' off runnin' for the house.

One leg after another, I slowly return to 'self and race up to the house.

All 'round me is a bloody mess. Slaves runnin' free from the slave quarters. Some runnin' to the house to defend it. Wat' we weren't ready for was how many whites were livin' inside. As I watch, I see one white man runnin' out yieldin' a whip in one hand and a knife in another. He begins killin' some of our men!

I see him run left for a slave girl tryin' to escape for the tobacco fields ova' yonder.

"Get back ova' here!" I hear him shout at her as he is runnin' after her. After they are out of my sight, I grab a scythe layin' in front of me. I pick it up and run for 'em.

"CRACK!"

The whip cuts through the air to land 'cross her back. She stumbles to the ground face first. He catches up to her, and I catch up to both to get a first-row look. As she screamin' for help, he wrestles his way on top of her. Steady tryin' to drive the knife in her.

Not again... not again! I feel my legs and feet sink into the ground. All I can do is squeeze the scythe tighter in my hands. I know I need to run ova' and help her...

Legs! Move! Do somethin'! My mind is screamin' at my body but nothin' moves.

"Reagor! Go help her!" Will shouts at me, "Come on let's go!"

I turn my head. He can tell in my eyes I ain't gonna' be no help to 'em. He takes off wit' his hatchet and topples the white man. Now Will and the Overseer start wrestlin'. The woman freed, climbs on the back of the white man wit' his knife in her hands and begins to stab him all ova' his back. Will hits the man wit' his elbow so hard he falls backward. As they stand ova' him catchin' they breath, Will tells her to go find safety wit' the group. As she marches off, Will picks up his hatchet and hits the man three times in the chest. He jogs to me. I be in the same position he found me in. He shakes his head, leavin' me wit' my own thoughts.

No words need be said.

Mon. Aug 22, 1831 02:40 AM: Nathaniel Francis Plantation

"KNOCK! KNOCK! KNOCK!"

"Massa' Francis! Massa' Francis, Come quick!"

"KNOCK! KNOCK! KNOCK!"

Ryan, the Overseer, charges down stairs. He swings the door open wit' his gun at his side. "Who is it?! What you want?!"

"Sir, it's me Red Nelson,"

"Red Nelson? Boy, what you doin' up here?! And why you bangin' on this door like you crazy, we're trying to sleep,"

"Sir, I need to speak to Massa' Nelson quick fast! It be 'bout his sister Mrs. Sally,"

"He ain't here, him and his Momma headin' down to Sally's after supper. Didn't you see them? What's wrong?"

"Sir, they done killed Mrs. Sally and Mr. Joseph Travis!"

"What?! Who killed 'em?! The British?"

"No Sir, it be some niggers from the plantation! Nat and a whole bunch of 'em. Yesterday they done killed Massa' Travis and Mrs. Sally in the big house, then they marched onto other places. I hid out 'cus I was scared. When I saw fit it be safe to leave, I headed to Massa' Salathiel Travis house, but they been there too and killed him and the white folks there! So I came runnin' up here!"

"Oh my God, you ain't lyin' boy is ya?!"

"No, Sir, I loved Mrs. Sally and Massa' Travis. They was better to me than any other,"

"Okay, well Nathaniel and his Momma is headed down to Sally's, so they should be there or be there soon. Once they see what happened, they will get the word out for help. Meanwhile, we need to-"

Ryan stares off at the dark of night in the distance. If you weren't lookin' all would seem still, but the night seem to be closing in. The night started to have shimmers flickering throughout. Wit' the footsteps of the group chargin' forward, Ryan knew what he was seeing.

Shoving Red Nelson in the house, "They're here! Go inside, hide the boys and Luvenia in the short wall upstairs. I'll do my best to fend them off.

Wit' his gun drawn, Ryan runs towards the moving night.

Red Nelson watches for a spell, then races up the stairs to try and get to Ms. Luvenia. Making his way up, he stops off in the first room to find the Brown boys sleepin' away in they bed. Red Nelson locks the door from the inside. Prayerfully they'll be quiet 'nuff to keep 'em safe. He charges down the hall to the Master bedroom. He looks in to see Luvenia. What Red Nelson didn't know is she be eight months pregnant.

"Ms. Luvenia.... Ms. Luvenia, wake up! Wake up now!" Red Nelson shouts at her while shovin' her to wake up. Red Nelson has survived slavery long enough to know he shouldn't be putting his hands on a white woman, but circumstances call for desperate measures.

"AHHH!!!" Ms. Luvenia screams.

"Please, please calm down! It's me Red Nelson. Look, there's no time to waste! Some niggers are on they way to come kill ya'! You best get movin' and go hide!"

"What?! Oh my God... Ryan! Ryan!"

"Ma'am he outside fightin' right now, he told me come hide ya' please we best get movin,"

Red Nelson helps Luvenia out of bed. No time for extra clothes for the voices of the insurrection was gettin' louder.

When the house got its addition on the second floor, it became a story and a jump type house. Yet with that change down the hall, it created a short wall. So if danger ever came, they could go and hide out 'til the danger passed.

Quickly, Red Nelson helps Luvenia shuffle down to the end of the hall and open the door to get her in the room. She slowly gets down to try and wedge her and her belly in the small space. Once she's able to get in she turns back to Red Nelson,

"Oh my God, Wait! The boys! I forgot the boys, where are they?!"

"It's okay, I done locked them away too! Please get on up in there! I'mma' go try and steer 'em away."

Shutting the door, he races down the stairs and heads for the back door. He starts knockin' some stuff ova' to make it seem like Luvenia escaped out the back. After swingin' open the back door, the front door opens quickly and slams shut. It's Ryan fallin' to the floor.

Red Nelson rushes back to give his help.

"Where's Luvenia?" Ryan asks.

"I put her up and away Sir. Sir we gotta' get ya' some help!"

"I never seen so many niggers in my life! Why they doin' this to us?!"

"Sir... Sir, let's get ya' some help!" Red Nelson pleads with him as the blood pool 'round Ryan grows.

"Where... What about the boys? Where they at?" Ryan asks whil' coughin'.

His answer is standin' on the stairs behind them.

"Ryan... why are you bleeding? Where's Mommy?" The older Brown of the Brown boys asks.

Ryan grabs Red Nelson by the collar and pulls him in close to him real violent.

"I thought I told you to hide them?! What are they doing out?!" Ryan shouts.

Red Nelson answers, "I don't know, Sir. I locked them up in they —"

BANG! Went the front door!

They're here!

"Get away from him Red! Wait! Wat' you doin' here?!" Will shouts at Red Nelson whil' holdin' up his hatchet. Men and women wit' him pour in from the back and front of the house.

"I came up and... I uh, tried to come up and find y'all. I saw some white folks was comin' for y'all and wanted to help ya." Red Nelson gives as his reason.

Will looks over at bloody Ryan on the floor and the two little boys 'round him.

"Hey Will looka' here, don't kill 'em. Let's move on ya' know? Let's let them live this day, please?"

"Wat' you know 'bout livin'?"

"Huh?" Will barks at Red wit' offense takin' to the plea.

"I say, wat' you know 'bout living? You ain't never lived a day here. They don't let ya' live. Now, when we get to feel wat' livin' be like ya' want us to stop! I say no! They gotta' die!" Will shouts while starin' down at Ryan holdin' on to the two boys. Their hate for one another is evident.

"Please, Will! Look at me! Don't do 'dis here. Y'all ain't gonna' do nothin' but make it worse for all of us. They gonna' start killin' even more of us wit' more hate than ever before! Is that wat' you want?"

"Please..." Red Nelson pleads wit' Will.

"My life means as much to me as any man. My freedom means as much to me as any man. Yet this man and men like him fight to keep freedom, to keep my life away from me. I'm willin' to die for all these people to have they life and have they freedom. If that means they get sent on to glory sooner than they want... so be it!"

With his short handle, big bladed hatchet, Will slew all that was white before him. Small and old.

A loud thud echoed from upstairs.

Followin' that, the last screams and cries fell. Red Nelson fell to his knees, wept.

As the house is ransacked, Will asks Nelson,

"Where's the rest of 'em?"

"They not here."

"Red, where they at?"

He looks at Will wit' tears in eyes. "I said, they ain't here. Massa' Francis and Ms. Luvenia was gone when I got here. All that was here be these three."

"Mhm.. we gonna' see." Will responds while lookin' 'round the house.

Will grabs a young lad, "Come here, go on upstairs and look up in the rooms and in the cubby space for any white folks."

"Yessir," the boy says before runnin' upstairs.

As seconds pass, Will and Nelson stay put in silence while they waits for upstairs's findings.

After some time, the lad comes back downstairs to offer up his findin's,

"There be no one upstairs, Sir."

"Ya' sure?"

"Yessir, the beds upstairs be empty, and when I looked in the cubby, I reached my hand far inside but couldn't touch anything."

"Okay,"

The young boy runs off wit' the rest as they exit the house 'til Nelson and Will are left.

"Well, I be seein' ya' Nelson. In this life or the next, we shall see."

"Yes... we will."

21
WE HAVE A PROBLEM - MON. AUG 22, 1831
06:20AM

"Sir looks like more have arrived," Thomas spoke to get the attention of Mayor James Trezevant.

Mayor Trezevant pokes his head out abruptly from the cluster of whiteheads. Around his desk are a group of angry white men frantically assessing the situation from his table with madmen surrounding him.

"More? As in more have escaped, so that means they have killed more of us! Damnit!"

"Where are this group from!? More importantly, where are they going?!" Mayor Trezevant loudly asks as the panic room stops for a moment to listen to the conversation.

"Yes, Sir, they are survivors from the Francis Plantation. It looks like the nigger revolt is moving West.

"Good Lord, these poor souls! Okay, listen up everyone," Mayor Trezevant steps out and walks towards the middle of the room. "We need to head them off at the pass. I need strategies! We need answers on how to handle this situation. Far too many whites are dying and we need to solve this before panic breaks out all ova' the county!"

"Thomas, with me." Mayor Trezevant says as he points in Thomas' direction.

Mayor Trezevant quickly storms out of the room to make his way down to the foyer. As Mayor of Southampton County, the people expect him to do his job. That's to protect and serve the people. Needless to say, he is responsible for getting into the dirty work when the situation calls for it. Speeding down the spiral staircase, Mayor Trezevant greets the survivors at his doorstep with a warm embrace.

"I'm so glad you were able to travel and make it to safety. Please let me be the first to offer my apologies and assurance that as your Mayor, I take my responsibility seriously, and I will see to it that you receive the justice you deserve. You will be vindicated for the hardships you have endured this evening. No person should have to suffer and see the things you have. Please, follow Eric into the back room where you will be served and comforted."

Mayor Trezevant gestures Eric over, "Eric, lead these people to the back, please. See to it they are taken care of."

"Yes Sir. Please this way." Eric directs them in a comforting way.

As they walk to the back, Mayor Trezevant watches them, allowing the situation's empathy to guide his next statements.

"Thomas, that could have been any of us. This is a terrible situation we are in."

"Yes Sir, yes it is."

"Did they have any information about their leader?"

"No Sir, just like the others, all they could say is they seemed organized and were blood-hungry as if possessed by the devil."

"These niggers are troubling pieces of property. They will know their actions have consequences." Turning to face Thomas, "We must see to it that justice is served. They expect me to uphold that law I studied for so long. I intend to."

"Yes Sir. I know you will. So what do you feel we should do next?"

"Let's get a drink."

Mayor Trezevant and Thomas walk towards the study to the right of the house. There is a table with pristine crystal glassware with the finest bourbon. Mayor Trezevant pours a glass for Thomas and hands it to him. He then pours one for himself and walks towards the neighboring seats. He gestures to Thomas to take the chair across from him. Mayor Trezevant begins to take sips out of his glass, staring off into the stillness of the water on the table. The last five hours have been chaotic, stealing a few moments of tranquility is needed to muster up the necessary strength to fight the good fight against these niggers.

"Has that house nigger Johnny confessed yet?"

"No Sir, no word there yet from the police Captain. He has been sticking to his story about coming to let us know as soon as the incident became apparent."

"Well keep me posted. He could be telling the truth since all these survivors have been coming, but I think he knows more than what he thinks he does. Please don't kill him. We gotta' get this situation under control. Too much innocent blood has been spilled. Even just one dying at the hands of a nigger is unacceptable. We must gain back our rightful place and them knowing their place, as the good Lord intended it to be."

Standing up to walk to his desk, Mayor Trezevant slumps into his chair and spins slowly left and right while sipping his bourbon. After a moment he speaks,

"Thomas, take note this is what we are going to do."

Thomas places his glass on the table and hurries to stand in front of the desk for direction. "Yes Sir?"

"Send word to William Broadnax. Tell him to assemble his men, and some local militiamen will meet him at the last sighting. Tell him to handle it by any means necessary."

"You sure Sir? Some owners won't like that their most valuable assets have come up dead."

"We will handle that at a later time. The bigger purpose is not to appear weak. In order to keep the standard of life created and not have this serve as a symbol, we must act in kind."

"I need an updated count on how many victims there have been thus far."

"Very well, Sir. Should we send a hurried word to Governor Floyd in Richmond?"

"Get me the information I requested, and I'll pen our official message myself."

Aug 22, 1831 06:45 AM: Execution: Captain Barrow

I don't know much 'bout Captain Barrow, but the one thing I know is, he is the man slave owners send they unruly slaves to for breakin'. He's the stalwart of Southampton County servin' in the War. This will be our first test.

"This ain't gonna' be easy, Nat," Sam says softly to Nat.

"True, but the challenge will aid us in the challenges to come."

"We also need to survive this here challenge to make it to the' next one. And 'dis man served in the War."

"We will. And if we don't, we don't. At least we broke the shackles to get to our challenge. Since there is no cover all we can do is move wit' haste. Will and Hark, go 'round back wit' some men, find a way from behind. I'll ride in wit' the others on the horses and guns."

"Yes, Sir," Hark answers to Nat's order.

As Hark starts walkin' away, Nat grabs his arm and turns him 'round,

"There will be slaves that fight against us. Do ya' best not to kill them, yet protect yaself at all costs."

Hark nods his head in agreein' before walkin' ova' to Will and shares the orders given. One by one, I see men picked by Will and Hark to follow them. I can see their bravery shine brighter than the fadin' moonlight. I know they won't pick me. I'm sure Will has told them 'bout me by now. Here I am sittin' wit' the leaders, and I can't move when someone in trouble need me.

I start weavin' through the men and women to stand in the back wit' some of the horses and wagons. I thought it best for all 'dat I make my way to the back. Angry wit' myself, I grab a sword layin' in the weapon wagon and start swingin' at a tree.

As I swing wit' all my might, back and forth at the tree, I feel a firm grip on my shoulder. I quickly turn 'round,

"Reagor. I want ya' wit' me, son." Nat said.

I give no words. I stand hangin' on to my sword wit' my head low.

"Wat' is it?" Nat asks.

"I'm... I'm not so sure that's a good idea." I mumble.

"Why?"

"I'mma waste. I'll be in the way. I'm too young to be up wit' the leaders. I'm no leader. I got too scared last time to do anythin' but look 'round. Wat' if..."

"Wat' if, wat'?"

"Wat' if I get scared again and someone dies 'cus of me, or runs free, or I die?!"

Nat walks towards me and places his hands on my shoulders. I struggle to lift my head to look at him, so he lifts my head for me.

Nat pours into me, "A leader is not the greatest killer. Killin' is easy. It can be done for selfish reasons. A leader is somethin' else. Part of a leader is willin' to place others in front of yaself, for their benefit. I have faith in ya'. Have faith in yaself."

He walks a few steps ahead of me and stops. He looks over his shoulder. I can see he's waitin' on me to choose. I walk to him and then we walk side by side where the men on horses are waitin'.

I jump on the last horse in the back of the line as Nat presses on to walk to the front to get on his horse.

"Men have faith in who you are! We ride to fight to get one step closer to our freedom. One step closer to our divine destiny! The Lord will order our steps, be not afraid, but be full of strength and joy!"

Wit' all the victories we seen how could you not believe.

We ride our horses to the battle awaitin' us. Even though I'm in the back, the closer we get, the more my heartbeat grows in my chest, matchin' wit' the feet of the horse under me. I was ridin' and prayin' I'd pick up my courage along the way or at least leave my fear behind me. The closer we get, we see and hear the assembly of Captain Barrow and his men. Wit' 'bout a half-mile between us, we see Captain Barrow and the other whites call they slaves out to get 'em in line in a hurry. They had skill on their side. The only thing I could hope for is our will and great numbers take 'em ova'.

"BOOM!" "BOOM!" "BOOM!" "BOOM!" "BOOM!" "BOOM!"

Shots ring out all 'round me! Captain Barrow's men and slaves are shootin' they guns at us. Not able to ride and shoot at once, I see our men get hit.

"Charge onward! Spread out!" I hear an echo from the loud voice of Nat and others.

Men are fallin' to the ground, horses begin to turn theyselves 'round to keep livin'. I see a few men steer they horses to the dark parts seein' it as a passage to safety.

Just get there! I think to myself as I press forward on my horse stayin' steady as one.

Finally, many of our militia make it to the gate of Captain Barrow's grounds. Nat leads the men to fight bravely! Even wit' the lack of skill, our courage and large numbers are helpin' us win.

I make it to the gate, jump off my horse, quickly throw the reins onto a post, and draw my sword. As I make my way, I sees many of our men layin' on the ground from being shot. Some are slaves of Captain Barrow. The men and slaves wit' Captain Barrow prove to be our biggest obstacle as Nat had said.

I begin marchin' forward carefully, wildly turnin' every which way I hear a sound. I see some of our men run that way chasin' some whites wit' some slaves to the left of the house. I quickly run behind 'em to give some help. As I'm runnin' I hear loud shouts in the distance.

"AHHHH!"

Quickly followin' the chant was Hark, Will, and their group of men peelin' out the woods stormin' the big house from behind, front, and sides. I took in a deep breath, hopin' I could catch some of the courage they put in the air. I run wit' purpose to the group fightin' round the barn side.

Twelve against five. Surroundin' in the inner circle was the two white men wit' they swords out. Protectin' them was three slaves wit' they weapons drawn tryin' to guide they Overseers to safety. Every time one of our men would take a swipe at the white men they block the attack.

Nat was clear, not to hurt any of our own if possible. The group keeps up the circle dance. I creep up the side and hide 'til the just time.

"Stay away! Stay back!" One slave yells out.

"Can't do 'dat. They gotta' die. We takin' our freedom now! Join us! Fight wit' us."

"No! 'Dis here is my Massas' and we won't let ya' harm them!"

"Get 'em boy!" One white man says pushin' one of the slaves encouragin' him to swing."

As the warfare dance goes on, I eye an openin'!

Go! Go! You can do this! I shout in my head to get my legs to go runnin' as fast as I can. I quickly take the space and lunge into one of the slaves' back and knock him to the ground.

"No!" He screams out, fallin' to the ground. Soon after, the twelve swarms the others takin' the white man's life and pullin' him away from the negroes who fail at protectin' his life.

"Where dat' other one?!" Someone shouts out. I roll ova' to get back on my feet standin' at the ready wit' my sword attached to my hand as if it was part of me. The slave I knocked down slowly stands up to his knees holdin' onto a bloody sword that went through the body of the other Overseer.

Wit' tears in his eyes he shouts at us, "Look wat' ya' done made me do?!"

"No need to fear! We come to free you, not harm you. All of you, please join us." One of the twelve says.

"You don't get it. They will come. If not tonight. On the 'morrow, or the day after. They will kill us all for ya' sins!"

"Fight wit' us so that don't happen." He pleads.

Hangin' his head low, he begins to sob. I can't tell if they be tears of joy or tears of pain. Soon he lifts his head and looks at us,

"You don't get it. I'd sooner sit up at the feet of the devil than live to endure the sufferin' 'dey will put me through. Lawd, I pray ye' accept my spirit and forgives me!" As he looks to the sky and closes his eyes, he done strikes his heart wit' his sword. In his death, he lay his body on top of the Overseer's body just to keep it safe in death.

Wit' the weight of his spirit leavin' it kept us all still. I can't help but think what could he have been through to believe the sureness of death was better than fightin' for potential freedom.

"Do the rest of you wish the same fate? Choose different, I beg ya'?"

The other two slaves look at each other for a second.

They rise to they feet and answer, "We will go wit' ya'."

As we march back to the big house, we hear cheers of victory from the just freed and the winners. Many start dancin' out the house wearin' jackets, shoes, pants only befittin' of a white man. Yet we was free; no difference stood between us. Many were busy comin' out the house stackin' weapons, tools, food from the harvests, and bourbon. Lots of bourbon. Lookin' 'round I count more than thirty-five free men have joined us.

"Men, collect wat' we need then we need to go out and bury our dead for they fought a brave fight for us to see this victory," Will cries out to the group bringin' order and focus to the place.

As Hark and some peel off to explore the barns and sheds, Will leads some out wit' shovels. I notice Nat is missin'.

I wander into the big house, takin' my time as I gather wat' exactly goes into a big house. 'Side from the broken items and bloodstains everywhere, the home had the best in it wit' nice chairs, big high ceilings wit' lights hangin' from 'em. Fancy rugs are layin' on top of the wood floors. It's meant to be like the person that live in it. I make my way through the house and hear grunts comin' from outside the back of the house. I peek 'round. I see Nat wit' a shovel diggin'.

I stand in the comfort of the house as I see Nat dig away.

He measures how deep the hole is, 'den begins to climb out and disappears to his left for a short whil' pullin' somethin' from the side.

At first, I had the feelin' to step out and help, but I wait in my spot to see wat' he is draggin'. Once he get to the hole, he uncovers Captain Barrow's body.

He slowly rolls him inside, and kneels ova' the grave, and begins to talk to himself. I can't make out wat' he sayin' 'cept when he stands to his feet. I hear an "Amen," leave his lips. He then starts layin' the dirt on top.

22
Secret Short Wall - Mon. Aug 22, 1831 07:00 AM

"Nathaniel?...Nathaniel?" murmurs Luvenia as she awakens.

Springing up from the cold wooden boards, she grasps her belly as she tries to steady her racing breath and heart.

"Oh, my head!" she thinks to herself. She reaches to examine her head and feels her hair matted together on the left side. As she feels around, she looks at the planks where her head was and sees a small, still pool of blood. Recognizing where she is, she tries to recall what happened with little luck, but clearly, something terrible has happened if she's seeking refuge in the cubby. Luvenia shuffles her way to the front of the cubby hole; somehow she got farther back than she's ever been. She opens the door with trepidation. A chilling breeze from outside pierces through Luvenia's body causing her to pause before stepping out. Things feel wrong, very wrong.

"Chile, I'mma take 'dis here dress!" Charlotte shouts to Ester across the bedroom.

Pausing with a smirk of confusion, Ester turns towards Charlotte, "Now wat' you gonna' do wit' Ms. Luvenia's weddin' dress?! Watch you gonna' find yaself get caught. All dat's gonna' do is cause attention to yaself."

"I ain't gonna' wear it! I'mma sell it or make somethin' out of it. I don't know wat' I'mma do wit' it, all I know is it's mine now, and I can do wit' it whatever I darn well please!"

Charlotte holds the dress up to herself and hugs it, "Mmhm! Ester, did you hear me?! A slave. Takin' ownership of somethin'. For myself!"

"Yessum, I heard ya,"

"Feels good, don't it! All we done ever got ta' own was the lashes, aches, pains, and brandin's. Praise the good Lawd, dem' white devils got wat' they been needin'! They can own that Death. I don't want that."

"Massa' Francis wasn't here fo' all 'dis which is a shame. I didn't mind Ms. Luvenia. She was da' kindest to me. I'm just happy I can get some clothes to cover up while I break fo' freedom," Ester says while searching through Luvenia's dresser drawers across the room.

"I say good riddance to all of "em! You find any money ova' there? You know we can't get nowhere wit'out no money." Charlotte asks.

"Naw, keep lookin' in dat' there trunk. Massa' Francis, gotta' stash his-"

Ester's words halt by the white ghost that stands at the Francis bedroom entrance. Luvenia stood alive and shocked, watching and listening to the conversation her slave hands were having.

"Char-... Charlotte?" Ester manages to mutter out of her mouth.

"Wat' Chile? Why you ova' there whisperin'?"

"Look,"

"Wat', wat' you see—"

Charlotte catches up to the unspoken conversation. After a few moments, Charlotte, the boldest of the two, speaks to Luvenia,

"Ms. Luvenia? Dat' be you?"

"Yes Charlotte! What are you doing in my house! Let alone going through my things."

"You not dead?"

"No!"

"Well... you soon shall be!"

Charlotte, quickly shuffling her hands on the floor, picks up the scissors she knocked off the trunk earlier. Without hesitation, Luvenia ran out of sight to head down the stairs. Following behind her was Charlotte with the scissors on a mission. Trailing behind her was Ester. With a small headstart, Luvenia starts shuffling down the stairs as fast as a pregnant woman can. She makes it to the bottom. As she breaks left for the back door to head into the woods, she's deterred by the sight of the slaughter left behind.

"Oh precious God, No! Not the boys! No, no, no!" Luvenia shouts as she collapses to the floor. Slowly she corrals the soulless bodies of the Brown boys. Luvenia begins pressing her tearful face against their chilling cheeks. With every tear, she remembers what caused her to collapse in the cubby hole in the first place. Hearing the slaughter of a loved one should be a sound no one should be subjected to. Yet, to listen to the screams of two boys you've become a surrogate mother to, can rip the very breath from your body.

Reaching the bottom of the stairs is Charlotte and Ester. They stand there watching Luvenia weep ova' the Brown boys, realizing she did not know, let alone see them dead.

"Say ya' last goodbyes, Ms. Luvenia! You sho' gonna' see them soon."

Slowly lifting her head at Charlotte, "Do what you will then, Charlotte!"

Charlotte draws back her hand to strike, yet an opposing force grabs her arm and throws her down on the stairs,

"Charlotte, you can't do 'dis here! Don't kill her!"

"Wat' is ya' doin'?"

"Savin' Ms. Luvenia. Look at her! She done lost enough now. Don't do 'dis. God won't be pleased."

"Pleased!?" Charlotte shouts while getting on her feet.

"Why is you protectin' her?!"

"She been good to me, so I can be kind to her."

"Really?!, where was she when 'dey took my brother away, 'cus he couldn't work no mo'? Where she when Massa' Francis whipped me into da' ground 'cus I was movin' too slow and let the blood pour out 'til I fell out? Where was she when dat' good fo' nothin' Overseer came out and forcin' himself on us at night?! I lost mo' 'den enough! Even wit' her losin' her life, she still ain't losin' mo' than me!"

"I know, Charlotte. I know, but I just can't let ya' do this." Ester pleads.

"Well sista', Not much you can do 'bout it. I'mma just have to go through ya'. You'll thank me later!"

Ester and Charlotte lock arms with one another vying for position. Charlotte, fueled with anger, uses her size to shove Ester to the floor and out the way. Looking to shove the scissors into the heart of Ms. Luvenia, Charlotte is grabbed from behind again.

As she's thrown across the hallway, Red Nelson shouts,

"Gon' get outta' here, Charlotte!"

Mon. Aug 22, 1831 12:00 PM: Ms. Rebecca Vaughan's House

"Chirp -Chirp.... Chirp -Chirp... Chirp-Chirp" echoed through the woods.

Silence.

"Chirp -Chirp.... Chirp -Chirp... Chirp-Chirp" echoed again.

"Chirp -Chirp.... Chirp -Chirp... Chirp-Chirp" was then heard back.

"Let's go," Nat lets us know standin' still behind him. We march forward wit' luck on our side seein' Nelson, Henry, and Sam marchin' to us all wit' all they have.

"Good to see you well!" Nat says wit' a smile to the three men.

"It's good to see ya' too! Let me tell ya' I was thinkin' you'd never arrive, then I'd be left in charge to take us somewhere," Nelson says.

Both sides came together. The leaders make a bit of a circle and sit on the ground.

"How did it go?" Nat asked, startin' the sharin' of stories.

"It was scary! At first we thought we got lost goin' up there. Thank the Lord, Jack was able to get us back on track. We came up behind Massa' Blunt's plantation, which was a good thang. They was up and about by the time we got there. So we waited 'til they left and all lights went out. Will and Jack took a ladder from the shed and put it up on the house and climbed in through a window."

"Yeah," Will jumps in the story, "We went through the top window. We took off the shoes we had and walked on ova' to Massa' Blunt's room. It was him and his wife in there. I was so scared but I swung my hatchet and struck him 'cross his head. He woke up in a panic. Jack was able to kill the wife when she woke up and I then got my nerve and finished off Massa' Blunt."

"Good, good," Nat says, noddin' his head.

"After, we lit a lamp to let the rest know we finished and they went onto the land. There was only a handful of white men wit' a large number of slaves." Jack shares wit' the group.

"Good work men, good work. We too have had victory from our adversaries. We now have great numbers wit' us. We are close, so very close to our promised land." Nat says, allowin' some of his excitement shine through his calm.

"Reagor?" Nat calls.

"Sir?"

"I need you to count all we have in men, women, and children."

"Yes Sir."

"Let's get some rest and food before we press on. Our next stop is Parker's field. It be the last plantation before we reach Jerusalem."

We all disperse wit' a feelin' we never had before. Right before our eyes wit' our very hands we moldin' the prayers of our people into a hope that we are now puttin' to work. This hope runnin' through us all may get us to that promised land.

Aug 22, 1831 01:30 PM: Governor Floyd's Office

22nd August, 1831:

S°ampton County sct:

To Governor Floyd - Richmond.

Whereas the said County I preside over, it comes with great sadness to notify of an insurrection which has befallen our said County. It is unclear as to the slave(s), which lead them, but it is clear they are large in number. As of this day [22nd], there have been fifty-five deaths, including men, women, and children. There are suspected to be more. Within my power, I have dispatched a nobleman William Broadnax, who has battle experience. With the local militia awaiting his command, he will defend the citizens, end this insurrection, and bring the leader(s) to the jail of the said County, charging them with conspiring to rebel & making insurrection & killing innocent men, women, and children. It is unclear to say how large the insurrection is however, some of the victims that were fortunate to escape tell of large groups that they have ever seen.
We have reason to believe they were led to conspire against us. Two weeks prior we arrested one white male Northerner who was recognized and detained for interrogation. A negro woman from the North was later found and arrested three days after to wit' they both are under interrogation for further information. Also, a mulatto negro boy found his way to my estate, who is also being questioned for involvement or information.

I request you hold on dispatching help until further notice on our local militia's success or failure to defend our great people — at which time & place you are to attend — Given under my hand & seal this 22nd day of August 1831.—

JAMES TREZVANT J.P.

"Gather the militia. Put them on notice for 3,500 men to be at the ready to dispatch to Southampton County upon my word. I want a daily update as to what's happening." Mayor Floyd commands his aide.

23
DON'T SETTLE - MON. AUG 22, 1831 09:30PM

Marchin' along the plantation edges, I find myself lookin' to the sky and another beautiful moonlit sky catches me. Another nightfall is a silent witness to another slave victory. As we press on from Ms. Vaughan's House we make it to our rest place, Parker's Field. By grace, luck, or wisdom, we is able to take hold wit' lil' effort. Wit' each victory we gain more strength in us and our leader.

"Chirp -Chirp.... Chirp -Chirp... Chirp-Chirp" echoed through Parker's Field.

I begin to march on back to the big house. Lookin' 'round it's amazin' to see the numbers of freed slaves. Strong men and women made the choice to fight they way to freedom. Never deep in my soul would I believe we be still livin' after two days. Let alone whites dyin' at the hand of negroes for two days.

Standin' at the openin' of the door to the big house be Nelson, Will, Hark, and Sam. Standin' in the doorway be our General, Nat. As I'm makin' my way through the crowd, I see Nat wipin' the blood stains off his face. His clothes have really gone through the storm wit' his reign. No matter to him or any of us, our goal was bigger and better than some fancy clothes. Nat raises his hatchet high in the sky for all to be quiet and gather theys attention,

"Men! Give thanks for the Lord has given another victory in our hands this night! We are movin' as one. We've answered the call when the time came due. Reagor?! Where you be?"

I look up wit' my eyes wide as the moon. I slowly raise my hand from within the black sea of people. Nat gestures for me to come. Doin' so, I make my way through the crowd to meet him up at the stairs. As I'm walkin', he says, "Come up by me."

I stand next to him as he speaks to the crowd again, "Slaves of Parker's Field that have bravely decided like a free person to join us, please step up close."

I'm in awe of seein' how many people stepped forward versus the congregation's size that did not. We have grown in mighty numbers.

All was quiet to hear wat' Nat spoke to the newcomers.

"No more is you slaves. No mo'! Wit' us here, on this night, leave that behind. Leave that slave mind behind and pick up ya' humanity for that's ya' true identity. On this night before God and ya' brothas and sistas, you is free from bondage. Be strong and of good courage, do not fear nor be afraid of the white man. Together we be strong and we will lean on one another for safety in our journey to the promised land!"

"'Dis here be Reagor," Nat says while placin' his hand on my shoulder, "When we finish stay here. He needs to get a count for me."

"Nelson, Hark, Sam, Will?"

All four turns back to look at Nat.

"Be sho' to assign out jobs to the rest. Give out food and water. Search fo' supplies, tend to the wounded. Once completed, gather Will and Henry to meet me inside. Okay?"

"Yessir!"

The four men go down to the people and begin addressin' they orders. Nat turns to walk into the house, but 'forehand he puts his hand back on my shoulder and says,

"After ya' finish countin', go help them. Then join us inside, okay?"

I nod yes. Nat walks inside and disappears into the house.

I'm left standin' on the stairs of the house wit' a group of people starin' at me to where it seem they joint silence is screamin' at me, "Wat' you supposed to be doin'?!"

I take a deep breath and step up, "Okay... after I count ya' go on down to see Hark where you 'posed to go next."

I start wit' the woman to my left,

"Two - One - Nine... Two - Two - Zero... Two - Two - One..."

Aug 22, 1831 10:00 PM: Explorin' Upstairs

"Nat?!... Nat?!" I shout while enterin' the house wit' no response. I stood in the hallway for a minute lookin' 'round and my eyes land on the staircase goin' upstairs. I never been upstairs before. I look ova' my shoulders, but don't see anyone. So, I decide to mosey careful upstairs to see wat' be up there.

As I make my way up, I enjoy the moment from touchin' the smoothness of the wooden handrail to pullin' at the chipped paint on the walls. I'm decidin' wat' I wanna do right now, and it feels so good! Free roamin' in Massa's house is a big no-no. I'd be subject to a lash or two if I made the mistake of comin' into his house, let alone his upstairs wit'out his say so. Now look at me, takin' my time to do wat' I see fit.

Whil' on the second floor, I walk down the narrow hall and turn right to walk in the first room.

As I'm lookin' 'round, I see a wooden dresser wit' some drawers that be broken and others half-open as if someone went through them lookin' for somethin'. 'Cross the room is the grand bed wit' Mr. Parker still in it. His bareback facin' up. His blood is still fresh 'nuff to drip down his arm and onto the floor.

I move 'round the room as if I'm tryin' not to disturb him. I peek into his closet to see all the clothes kept in there. I grew tired siftin' through the number of clothes. Meanwhile, I'm still wearin' my old tattered shirt and shorts thrown at me by my Overseers. Gettin' more and more jealous wit' each piece of clothin', I stumble on a new white shirt that caught my eye. I pull it out and hold it up to myself in the shattered mirror next to the closet. After I look at myself in wat' could be, I look at myself as I am. Raggedy. I look back at Mr. Parker's dead body. I decide this here shirt will serve me better now that he won't be usin' it.

Mmhm.. I think to myself as I look at my new shirt. I begin to look at myself from all angles. I can't help but feel... happy? Joy? Is that wat' this is? Just puttin' on this shirt, I felt taller, stronger, bolder, freer. Then I thought to myself, *why stop here?*

I begin to poke through the rest lookin' for some pants and find some dark blue ones.

As I put 'em on and see the color more close, I can't help but think 'bout Momma. The color seem to favor her favorite dress. I understand the joy she felt wearin' that dress now. Wat' if I had these pants earlier, maybe me and her could wear both to church on Sundays and wear that joy together. I bet she be excited seein' me in these pants. Make 'em look all nice on me. I watch my tears fall thinkin' 'bout Momma.

"Lord, I pray Mommas' alright," I say. I walk back into the closet, wipin' my eyes to pull out this dark black coat tucked away in the front of the closet. It was so heavy for a piece of clothin'. I never thought the coats they be wearin' be this heavy. I put it on and button it up like I be seein' the Overseers do.

Mhm, 'dis here is a good coat!

While lookin' in the mirror, I happen to see a bloody handprint on the half closed door behind me. I turn 'round and walk to the door to explore. I push on the door but could only move it a lil' bit. It seems like somethin' is on the other side of the door.

I let out a few grunts of effort while pushin' to get the door to move. Finally, I was able to get it open 'nuff for me to squeeze through. Once I got through, I quickly fell to the floor.

Lookin' to my left had me layin' stiff. Up close was Mrs. Parker's lifeless eyes starin' at me. Her limp body was blockin' the door and cause me to fall. I quickly jump to my feet and angry start rubbin' at my new clothes tryin' my best to get the dust and blood off 'em. Seein' my efforts of rubbin' it was makin' it worse, I just throw up my hands. I begin lookin' 'round the room to see if they be some more closets for me to explore through but a small white crib against the far wall caught my eye first.

I step off to the side and look back and forth at the crib and Mrs. Parker. I walk up slowly on the crib and carefully place my hands on the bars to look inside and see that innocence didn't receive protection from our wrath this night.

I look back at Mrs. Parker and then back at the baby and can't help but feel woeful. I start to rub the coat up and down. In my secret sadness I feel the coat's warmth, comfort, and wet bloodstains. I start to unbuttonin' the coat. Turnin' to the crib, I lay the coat on top and wrap the baby in the comfort and warmth of the jacket since it couldn't have the comfort of its momma.

"Reagor!"

Turnin' to the door, I see Jack standin' wit' a jug of whiskey in his hand watchin' me.

"Wat' you doin' up here?"

I reply, "I, uhh- Nothin."

"Come on downstairs, we all waitin' on you." He mumbles as he takes another gulp before walkin' away.

"Yessir,"

I tap twice on the frame of the crib and walk away. I leave the room, and close the door to follow Jack down the stairs.

"I found him," Jack says to the room as he takes a seat in the kitchen area.

As I come 'round the corner to stand in the back, I try to offer my apologies to the room but is halted by Nat.

"Reagor, when I give an order, I expect you to follow it. Understand?"

"Yessir, but when I came in the house and shouted no one was here so I—"

"I didn't ask for ya' excuses. I asked if ya' understood me. Yes or no?"

Puttin' my hands down and clinchin' my fist behind me, I answer wit' a short, "Yessir."

"Good."

"Oh, give the boy a break! We, we is winnin' this thang here! No white man dare try to mess wit' us!" Nelson cheerfully retorts to Nat. His joy is comin' from his celebration bottle of bourbon.

"Here! Here!" Jack and Sam shout.

"Look! We here to meet a mission. To go forth in wat' we set out to do! We nearly three miles away from Jerusalem 'dis here is no time to celebrate." Nat says, tryin' to get the focus of his leaders back.

"Will, have we tended to the wounded?"

"Yessir, six killed in battle and one bled while we was tryin' to help him. All have been buried."

"Here, Here," Nelson adds before takin' a drink.

"Hark, wat' you find 'round for weapons?"

"They was some swords found. We got some more hatchets and three more muskets. Yet there ain't many bullets left fo' all the guns we got. I got some men goin' 'round tryna' collect, but so far no luck."

"Here, here," Jack follows up behind Nelson wit' a quick sip out of his jug.

"Okay, thank ya'."

"Reagor, wat' say you 'bout the total count?"

I reluctantly responded, "We at two-three-one."

"Thank ya'. Now, once all have eatin', we gon' march on out and head straight for the goal."

"Wait, wat'?! We not gonna' stay and rest?" Nelson shouts.

"No, it's only wastin' time when we can be ready to go in a short time and have victory in the mornin'," Nat rebuttals.

"But we are weary! Two days we been marchin' and killin' and marchin' and killin'. We made it thus far wit' lil' rest. We need to rest!"

"Look to me you doin' mo' drinkin' than restin' wit' wat' time you do have. So you sho' you don't wanna stay 'cus you wanna keep drinkin?"

Staggerin' to his feet, Nelson holds up his jug, "Wat's wrong wit' drinkin'?!"

"Here, here," Jack and Sam shout while laughin' before drinkin' some more.

"Drinkin' is wat' winners do. Drinkin' is wat' helped me get this far! I was drinkin' to hide my pain as a slave, but now I'm drinkin' 'cus I'm happy! Happy all these white folks is dead and we alive! I demand we stay! You not the only one that makes decisions. We all help, so we all should get to decide wat' we do!"

After Nelson's rant, Nat leans back in his chair and looks 'round the silent room. A mixed room of silence troubles Nat.

"Do you think you can make the tough decisions? Do you think you have the vision and respect to lead?" Nat says as he slowly stands to his feet, layin' his blood-stained hatchet on the table.

"Yes, I do." Nelson says wit' drunken strength.

"Fine. We shall see. Go 'head and make the call then. We shall see wat' follows."

Nelson answers back, "Well then, my decision is we stay the night here to sleep, eat, and be merry! Then in the mornin', we go forth to Jerusalem and kill every white person there!"

Nat takes in a long draw of air and then lets it out to get control of his anger. He picks up his hatchet to twirl it on the table.

"We are dismissed, men."

"Let's go," Nelson says to Jack and Sam while takin' a drawn out sip from his nearly empty jug. They both struggle to their feet and follow him out. Not before they pay respec' to Nat wit' a head nod.

Tues. Aug 23, 1831 01:45 AM: Parker's Field

"See anythin' we need to worry 'bout out there?" was a voice comin' from inside Mr. Parker's house. By the sound of it and the heavy footsteps, I could tell it's Nat. He comes and sits next to me, restin' on the porch.

"Waitin'... just waitin'..." I say soft, focusin' on the open land wit' scattered bodies. Some by death others by liquor.

"Waitin' for wat'?"

"Waitin' for mornin' to come, I guess. So we can move it along. Why, you up?"

"I haven't found it easy to sleep this last week myself. The work in front of us seems to keep sleep away from me."

I responded wit' a, "Mmhm," to allow for quiet to sit between us.

As I go ova' my countin' by numberin' the stars, my mouth starts to speak wat's on my mind, "You know I'm mad at you."

A small grin falls ova' Nat's face as he is lookin' at the sky too.

"Really? Felt I was mean to ya?"

"Yes! Wat' the hell was that 'bout? All this time here gettin' to know one another, and you decide to yell at me in front of errbody!"

"Weren't ya' given an order?"

"Yessir,"

"Didn't I before show ya' grace in your misstep?"

"Yessir,"

"Well then, Son, why do you feel it's ya' right to only be shown grace and praise? Did I cause ya' to mess up? Did anyone in that room 'cause ya' to disobey?"

"No, but I got a good reason for-"

"Son, everyone got good reasons for not doin' wat' they supposed to do. Or wat' they say they gonna' do. White folks gotta' good reason to lynch us all by our necks. White folks gotta' good reason for why we should be locked in shackles. Loose reasons ain't nothin' more than excuses. If we are to be better, we must hold each other to our word. Ya' word is a mirror of wat's in ya' heart. If we gonna' be justified and demand better of them, we first gotta' demand and protect better from one another before we expect better and defend better from our enemies."

Nat has a way of puttin' shame on ya' in a lovin' way.

"I'm sorry."

Nat walks up and gives me a hug like a father embracin' his son. "I been forgave ya', Reagor. Just got to forgive yaself and let it go!"

"Forgiveness?"

"It means to accept someone sayin' sorry in ya' heart when they do somethin' hurtful to ya'. Sometimes it's acceptin' the hurt someone did to ya' and movin' on even if they don't say sorry."

"Why would ya' do somethin' like that?"

"If ya' don't, then that person will always have power over ya'. There is power in forgiveness. You have to look inside to see if you can be strong 'nuff to forgive 'em."

"How hard is forgivin' somebody?"

"It can be harder than dyin'. God pushed me to forgive, and I had to prove that I was willin' to give forgiveness before He gave me the go-ahead to lead all y'all."

"So wat' you did earlier, was that forgiveness?"

"Wat' you mean?"

"I saw wat' ya' did back at Barrow's Farm. I saw ya' wrap up and bury Captain Barrow. Is that why you did that?"

"He deserved that type of respect and honor."

"He wat'?! Ya' know he shot at us, and done killed some of us too. Probably been killin' many of us before tonight. Why would you care wat' happens to him? I'm glad he's dead! You think he woulda cared 'bout you if he done killed ya'? He probably woulda hung us all, cut us into pieces, and showed it to all the rest of 'em."

"Respect and honor should be given to all. Don't matter if he would give it back or not, simply because we are equal. If all the killin' we are doin' and if all the people we are freein' is to mean anythin', it only means wat' we do in the dark! This ain't for revenge. I'm not tryin' to teach ya' to kill for pleasure. Revenge is poison that will kill you slowly. I'm leadin' us to demand justice and be justified in our reasons and actions. We must be willin' to accept wat' they refuse to accept in us."

"Like me and you, he had a life. That life means somethin', and he used his life to commit evil 'cross this land. God won't stand for it, and we shouldn't either. It's our duty to go forth and fight for justice, but we also must teach 'em where they went wrong for them to get back right in they hearts and minds."

"In that moment... when I was prayin' ova' him, I felt sorry for 'em. I also realized I am a leader. A true leader because of the weight of my voice and I'm learnin' to be skilled wit' one of the strongest weapons."

"Wat' that is?" I ask.

"True forgiveness. Wit' this weapon, I have been able to sever most of the pain I've endured. I'm severin' the sufferin' I've endured so that I can go forth and lead y'all wit' a clear vision to not only survive this fight, but we can heal together and thrive after this fight. A decisive victory is wat' my heart wants, not reckless death for the sake of death."

"Why? Why are you tellin' me this? How you know all this to be true?"

"Stick wit' me, for I promise to give you all that I've learned. I see you. I know you will lead people further than I can imagine."

My mouth shut wide open wit' his prophecy. Me, a nigger from the field ain't leadin' nobody, nowhere.

"I do owe you a 'sorry' though," Nat says.

"Why?"

"I lied as to why I came out here. I feel a shakin' in my spirit 'bout us restin' here is a mistake, yet I showed weakness at the meetin'. I let the fullness of the moment let us stay here. This is not our restful place."

"Well, I should say to you too, I'm sorry. I have been bothered by somethin' way back."

"Wat' that is?"

"Remember when y'all came and got me. As we rode off.... I saw my brother run off the other way and if I know him he's gonna' see 'bout gettin' revenge for killin' Mr. Mills."

"Mmmhm, I see. I see."

Nat stands to his feet and walks off the porch and paces for a while. I sit and watch.

After some time, he walks back over and says,

"Can you handle an order I'mma give you?"

I jump down to stand on my feet, "Yessir."

"I will go wake those who aren't drunk inside, go out and wake those out in the field and in the quarters. Meet me near the barn where the supplies are wit' haste."

"Yessir."

24
THREE BATTLES. TWO DIRECTIONS - TUES. AUG 23, 1831 02:30 AM

Thus far the insurrection been workin' 'cus, we been together tightly. Two - three- one slaves turned into freed negroes, wit' one mission led by Nat. We now down to one - three- seven. The rest lay scattered among the field and slave quarters drunk wit' bourbon and whiskey.

As usual, I find safety wit' the horses in the back, watchin' from far off. In the middle of the huddle, Will, Hark, and Henry are talkin' wit' Nat. The people stand weary awaitin' for some direction to either go back to sleep or get to work. Finally, one brave woman steps out and asks,

"Wat' is we meetin' fo'? Are we makin' a run for freedom?"

The leaders look at her and hurry to end they final words.

Nat gives a sign for all to be quiet as he walks forward to speak to everybody.

"Men and women, I call you here to share my angst. My spirit is gravely disturbed. So much that I must call on y'all, and we come to a decision."

"Those that are not here, decided to follow the leadership of Nelson and the other leaders. Their direction of leadin' you was to partake in strong drink and celebrate. Due to my mistake I allowed such to spread. No more! I have called you to follow me, fo' we will mount up and press forward to our true destiny, to our true rest place."

"Wat' say of the rest?" Someone from the group asks.

"It is hard to change the mind of a man when it's set in they way. When that happens, you must leave 'em to they own direction or force 'em to bend to ya' will instead of theirs. I will not force you to follow me. We have come thus far by those trustin' and believin' in me and my men. My heart is to succeed. I need you tho'. I need you to follow, I need you to fight, and most important, I need you to believe in the direction I'm leadin' ya'. If you feel the need to stay wit' the rest. Be merry in this place and be led another way, I will respect ya' choice."

"Nat, please can we -"

"Henry, enough! The call stands for ya' too. You either stay behind or go! I'm leavin'. Those that follow, will follow. Those that stay, will stay."

The chosen that woke when we gathered them came together and started talkin' 'bout wat's best.

"Will we take all the supplies wit' us?" Hark says.

"No, we'll take ours. They've fought wit' us to 'dis point. It's just to leave half of all that we've gathered wit' them and be helpful to their cause."

In my mind, I'd like to think I made it clear that up in 'dis here, horse and sword is comin' wit' me.

"Wat' say you?" Nat asks the congregation, "For we are to gather wat' is ours and leave now."

"We wit' you!" The group affirms their faithfulness to Nat.

"Good! Go collect, take half of all that is within the supplies and assemble to head off into the night."

The chosen acted. Nat turns back to the remainin' leaders. Henry's upset at the choice and he has choice words wit' Nat and the others. Nat and Henry keep goin' back and forth 'til silence falls ova' they circle. Nat reaches his hand out to Henry. Henry reaches out his and shakes. They break and go in separate directions. Nat walks in my direction.

"Reagor, I want to ride next to Hark. Will and I will lead on horseback." Nat says.

"Is Henry ridin' wit' the rest?" Tryin' to gain information on their conversation.

"Henry's not comin' wit' us. He is choosin' to stay wit' the others. He feels it best to stay wit' the rest and keep watch over 'em since they are not awake to do so."

"Oh,"

"So you gonna' take his spot. Is that okay?"

"Yessir."

"Good, let's get goin', no time to lose," Nat says as he walks away.

Thus far the insurrection been workin' 'cus, we been together tightly. Two - three- one slaves turned into freed negroes, wit' one mission led by Nat. At this moment, we are now down to one - three- seven. The rest lay scattered among the field and slave quarters drunk wit' bourbon and whiskey.

As usual, I find safety wit' the horses in the back, watchin' from afar. Amid the huddle, Will, Hark, and Henry are talkin' wit' Nat. The people stand weary awaitin' for some guidance to either go back to sleep or get to work. Finally, one brave woman steps out and asks,

"Wat' is we meetin' fo'? Are we makin' a run for freedom?"

The leaders look at the her and hurry to conclude the final statements.

Nat gestures all to be quiet as he walks forward to speak to the body.

"Men and women, I call you here to share my angst. My spirit is gravely disturbed. So much that I must call on y'all, and we come to a decision."

"Those that are not here decided to follow the leadership of Nelson and the other leaders. There direction of leadin' you was to partake in strong drink and celebrate. Due to my mistake I allowed such action to spread. No more! I have called you to follow me, for we will mount up and press forward to our true destiny, to our true rest place."

"Wat' say of the rest?" Someone from the group asks.

"It is hard to change the mind of a man when it's set in they way. When that happens, you must leave 'em to they own direction or force 'em to bend to ya' will instead of theirs. I will not force you to follow me. We have come thus far by those trustin' and believin' in me and my men. My heart is to succeed. I need you tho'. I need you to follow, I need you to fight, and most important, I need you to believe in the direction I'm leadin' ya'. If you feel the need to stay wit' the rest. Be merry in this place and be led another way, I will respect ya' choice."

"Nat, please can we —"

"Henry, enough! The call stands for ya' too. You can either stay behind or go. I'm leavin'. Those that follow, will follow. Those that stay, will stay."

The chosen that woke when we gathered them came together and started talkin' 'bout wat's the best choice.

"Will we take all the supplies wit' us?" Hark says.

"No, we'll take ours. They've fought wit' us to 'dis point. It's just to leave half of all that we've gathered wit' them and be helpful to their cause."

In my mind, I'd like to think I made it clear that up in 'dis here, horse and sword is comin' wit' me.

"Wat' say you?" Nat asks the congregation, "For we are to gather wat' is ours and leave now."

"We are wit' you!" The consensus affirms their allegiance to Nat.

"Good! Go collect, take half of all that is within the supplies and assemble to head off into the night."

The chosen acted. Nat turns back towards the remainin' leaders. Henry's upset at the choice and he has choice words wit' Nat and the others. Nat and Henry continue to share in their banter until silence fell amongst their circle. Nat extends his hand to Henry, to which Henry shakes. They break and go in separate directions. Nat walks in my direction.

"Reagor, I want to ride next to Hark. Will and I will lead on horseback." Nat says.

"Is Henry ridin' wit' the rest?" Tryin' to gain information on their conversation.

"Henry's not comin' wit' us. He is choosin' to stay wit' the others. He feels it best to stay wit' the rest and keep watch ova' 'em since they are not awake to do so."

"Oh,"

"So you gonna' take his spot. Is that okay?"

"...Yessir."

"Good, let's get goin' no time to lose," Nat says as he walks away.

OUTSIDE PARKER'S FIELD - 05:15 AM:

"Sir, all points are surrounded." says the runner.

"What of the back to the woods?" General Broadnax asks.

"Men have been placed with dogs at the ready. They won't get loose that way, sir."

"Good. We will begin our ascent from the east side, where the dew is rising, to give us as much cover as possible. Once we give the signal, the rest should press forward to squeeze them in and pick them off. Mayor Trezevant wants the leaders and some of the runaways captured. However, if you feel in danger or fear one to escape, don't hesitate to kill on sight." General Broadnax said to the runner.

As the runner goes off on his horse, General Broadnax turns his horse to survey the anger-filled faces of his fifty-piece militia. Like a sound orchestra awaiting their conductor's instruction, they steadily wait for direction to play to the tune of their song of destruction.

"Gentlemen. Our way of life has been threatened. Precious Americans have died on this soil by the hands of some wretched niggers! They seem to have mistaken our God-given kindness for weakness. One white dying was enough for the whole Virginia militia to come down and inflict justice, but more than fifty-five of our fellow citizens have died a senseless death by the hands of property that has gone awry. Keep that close to your heart! Go! Go forth and achieve victory and justice to restore the balance to our fair land!" Like a conductor that calmly taps his stand then slowly raises his arms high with his conductor's stick to garner the attention of his orchestra, General Broadnax draws his sword. He lifts it high in the air, and pulls it down to unleash the symphony of men and horses to fill the air with a symphony of gunfire, piercing screams, and death.

CYPRESS BRIDGE - 05:15 AM:

"Sir, all have safely crossed." Hark tells Nat.

"Wat' say you of the town, is all quiet?" Nat asks.

"Yessir. Two have traveled in town and back sayin' not much is there. At the armory, there are sounds of trainin' goin' on."

"Good. We will begin the fight from here. Will, you take twenty men wit' ya' and travel northwest of Jerusalem. Hark, you will take twenty men wit' ya' and travel northeast of Jerusalem. Once ya' travel 'bout a quarter mile from town, come back southward fast to offer aid. Head for the armory. May God be wit' you!" Nat orders the leaders. They head off quickly wit' they militia into the woods. The large group left, filled wit' men and women await directions. Nat takes in a deep breath of the light air, draws his sword, and speaks,

"Free negroes! This be the time for which we must be victorious like those of Israel we've learned so much 'bout. In they quest for justice, for freedom, God was wit' 'em. That same God be wit' us today! We won't scatter, we won't flee! March forward wit' courage in ya' hearts and ya' weapon in ya' hands. Take ova' the armory, take ova' the town wit' ya' brothas and sistas by ya' side. All of us here as one, be they biggest fear in the flesh!"

Each word fallin' off his lips rings through our ears an' darts fast into our soul! The poundin' of our hearts unites. The spirit under one cause becomes a wildfire, lit to overcome our sufferin' and leave behind our most wanted gift, freedom!

We run to go get it!

We run fo' Jerusalem!

TOWN OF JERUSALEM - 05:25 AM:

"Take Jerusalem! Freedom be restored!"

Nat continues to chant while ridin' fast on his horse leadin' us through town. Those on foot would echo the same chant while usin' they weapons to storm through the homes and stores through town.

I feel my heart in my hand. I keeps sayin' them words louder and louder. As they leave my lips, I feel my strength grow more and more. I feel my mind focus. Up ahead, two white men be crouched in the street wit' they guns drawn. I'm up against gunfire. Yet, for some reason in all the feelins' I had goin', fear wasn't one.

As my horse and I hasten toward the men, we become one in movin' from left to right, right to left wit' a grace 'dats so beautiful. Four hundred steps away became three hundred; then two hundred, then eighty. Wit'out thinkin', I hold out my sword tight on my right side. No sooner that man's head came clear, my sword sliced him 'cross his neck! Runnin' past him, I look back ova' my shoulder to watch his body fall.

Turnin' my horse 'round, I got a perfect view of the other white man tryin' to help the other I just killed. I look at my blade and wipe off the thick blood left behind on my shirt. I thought to myself, *Again!*

I yell, "Yah!", kickin' the sides of my horse to let her loose!

I race down to the man and hold out my sword. As we run 'dis time, I'm able to look at 'em dead in his eyes. My horse and I move down swift to catch 'em crouched tryin' to reload after a missed shot. In a slow blur, my horse brings me close 'nuff to where my blade comes 'cross his neck smooth. I see the tears racin' down his face 'fore the outpour of blood covered 'em up. Slowin' up my horse, I turn her 'round and 'cross the way, I see the bodies laid on top of one another.

Scattered all 'round be a crazy whirlwind. The ground is bein' painted a deep red wit' white and negro bodies 'round. The air is heavy. Wit' every breath, ya' taste the gunpowder. In all 'dis though, there are more whites laid out than negroes.

"Chirp -Chirp.... Chirp -Chirp... Chirp-Chirp"

"Chirp -Chirp.... Chirp -Chirp... Chirp-Chirp", rang like the tower bell through the land. Stormin' out of the buildings 'round me be negro men and women given all they got in they legs to race forward.

"The Armory!" they shout!

My horse and I get goin' to help!

PARKER'S FIELD - 06:00 AM:

"Ahhh!"

"Sir, no, Sir, please I'm sorry they done tricked my mind to —"

"Shhh.... Boy! No beggin!" I hear shouted in the distance. "You goin' straight to hell for what you did and ain't no stoppin' this!"

I hear some more pleas follow. Then end wit' a death silence.

Wat' started as dew has changed into a thick fog. You can't see but more than two feet in front of ya'. The only thing my mind could do was make out those be black bodies layin' in front of me. The other part of my mind was still too liquored up.

Lookin' up in the fog, there was shimmers floatin' through that seem to put my heart at ease for the moment.

I heard the words, "Die! Die! You worthless nigger!" ring out in the distance in front of me.

"Open up ya' mouth boy, I say!"

I try my hardest lookin' 'round, but my eyes can't make out the faces. The best I can do is make out shadows attackin' shadows. The sound of screams be comin' in late. Guess even in 'dis fog it's hard for sound to get through. One thing fo' sure, I can tell it be the screams of the people that stayed wit' me at Parker's Field.

Breathe... Focus on breathin' Nelson! I thought.

They done tied my hands behind me and placed 'em shackles back on my feet. They didn't even hurt when they put 'em on. I still had the marks on my skin from the last time I had 'em on. Hangin' my head low, so many thangs start runnin' through my mind! Each time it gets too foggy I just think to myself,

Breathe... Focus on breathin'! I say to erase my mind.

As time be passin' by, and more screams ring out I start lookin' to my left and right. The more I focus the more I can make out the faces.

I turn to look at Jack on the left, our eyes lock. I look right and there be Sam and Henry. Lookin' at they faces and bodies made me realize my body hurt. That bourbon is wearin' off more and more.

My soul is hurtin' the most. This be where I had led them. My leadin' led us into death.

I look up and straight in front be a figure of a man wit' his arms folded wit' a hat on gettin' closer. The closer it got to us, the faster I breathed.

Breathe... Focus on breathin'!

"Well, well, well. Good Morning to the special niggers! How you this fine morning?" General Broadnax asks.

We choose not to speak.

"Mmhm, they must not have heard me, men. Maybe I need to get a little closer," General Broadnax says wit' an angry smile.

Kneelin' in front of me, he smiles wide and puts his hand on his side. The more sober I get the more fear grows.

"AHHH!" I scream out loud. Bein' stabbed in the leg will get ya' to scream.

"Nelson!?" Jack yells ova' to me. Wincin' in pain all I can do is breath aloud.

"You shut your filthy mouth you special nigger!" General Broadnax yells at Jack while pointin' in his face. General Broadnax stands there whil' a frightenin' smile slowly comes 'cross his face. The sight of it was too much for ya' eyes.

"Now all of you, I asked you a question. Don't ya' think it's rude not to answer?!" He sharply says while shakin' the blade lodged in my leg.

"YESSS SIR!" I force outta' me.

"Good! Now, let's try that again! How are you this fine morning?"

"Good, Sir!" We all shout to be heard clearly.

"That's good to hear!" He says as he stands back to his feet, pullin' the blade out wit' 'em.

He stands ova' me. He looks ova' his blade drippin' wit' my blood.

"Me, I'm not too good. I got an urgent letter that they was some special niggers down here stirring up some trouble like never before."

While wipin' his blade off on my shirt he keeps goin', "So me and my men was summoned down here to put an end to these special niggers that thought it be alright to start disrupting life, make a ruckus, and start killing poor innocent white folks. Now, nothing gets my boys and I upset like innocent white people dying, especially at the hands of a nigger. But I realized on our way down here. Y'all ain't just some regular niggers, y'all like to think of yaselves as some special niggers."

General Broadnax backs up so he can look at all four of us. Behind us I hear,

"No Sir, please! It wasn't my fault! Please don't kill me!"

"Shut up boy!"

"BANG!"

"In case you haven't realized, that is the sound of the niggers you tricked to work with ya' dying. See, the Mayor of this great town and the Governor have a problem. They want to stomp out this little insurrection you got going but see, y'all have killed more white people than ever in our fair loving state here. So, the good, wholesome, God fearing people that live here are going to require retribution for the problems you brought. They are going to want justice to be served. And they gonna' get it."

"AHHH! My arm! You done cut off my arm!" echoes from the distance.

General Broadnax kneels down and starts rubbin' the grass in front of him.

Breathe... Focus on breathin'! I think.

"I was talking with my men here and we feel it's only right we get a little more justice. We are owed that and the lives you took these last few days are owed more than that. Even in the good book it says an eye for an eye. So we're going to take some of you niggers' lives. Not just they lives though. We going to take some heads, some arms, some legs. And what we're going to do is hang 'em up all around this town to let these good white people know that the way things go, the established livin', is back to order. And to let your kind know that these here serve as a reminder that they don't ever, ever want to be special niggers. That it would make sense to go with the flow we have here."

I hear Henry softly say through his tears, "Dear Lawd, help us." My soul latches on to 'dat prayer.

"Now the only question I have for y'all. Y'all are the leaders of this here insurrection right? See my men found y'all laid up in Mr. Parker's house. So is it safe to say y'all leading this thang?"

I look to my right at Sam and Henry and then to my left at Jack.

I look straight at General Broadnax in the eyes and say,

"Yesir! We they leaders!"

General Broadnax grabs me up by the collar, and starts thrashin' my face wit' the butt of his sword. In between every word he declares,

"Don't - You - Ever - Look - me - in - the - eye!"

After throwin' my body to the ground General Broadnax stands up straight speakin' to his men,

"String up the rest of the bodies and limbs. 'Round up a few more of 'em then march them down to Mayor Trezevant place for them to serve their day in court. "

Layin' there on the ground, focusin' on my painful breaths, I can"t help but smile in the grass.

At least....

At this moment. I could be a leader.

THE ARMORY IN JERUSALEM - 06:35 AM:

"Commander, I don't think we can hold them off!" I yell.

"Keep fighting, Soldier! We will not give up ground. We are Jerusalem's last stand! The rest of the men are miles off fighting elsewhere." The Commander of Jerusalem yells back at me.

"But Sir, I think we should retreat!" I yell at the Commander trying to reload his gun.

The Commander yanks me by the collar, "Look! If we leave, we've lost Jerusalem. Do you understand!?"

"Sir, look around you; we are already losing. Men are dying! Jerusalem is falling!"

"Look out!" The Commander shouts while slinging me to the side.

With haste, I pick up my sword from the ground and run towards the facility's east side, where we train for assistance. All that was left was my fellow soldiers slain all ova'. I sprint for the front gate. Maybe I can escape to find some help left in town or find some men at the other battle.

The front gate is in shambles! The Commander is wielding his sword back and forth to ward off the eight slaves with scythes, axes, and hatchets pointed at him. They got him pinned down.

I slowly back up towards the wall behind me, trying to hold my sword steady in my hand with no luck. All around me are negroes killing white men with joy. Some of them are dying as well but not enough to regain control! All I want to do is serve my fair state of Virginia and be part of something that matters, that made a difference. I've only been in training for three weeks! Now here I am, thrust into a situation where I'm fighting and killing. I'm only nineteen for Christ's Sake!

I look back towards the gate and I see this young slave charge in on a horse with a sword in his hand. He has streaks of blood on his shirt. He looks to be no older than me.

I think to myself, *shit!*, after we lock eyes. I was praying to become invisible. He focuses on me and rides his horse towards me. The closer he gets, the sweatier my hands are. I became paralyzed to the reality that my very life is slipping away.

Through the chaos of my mind, one rational thought emerges.

I quickly toss my sword away and fall to my knees with my hands held high, "I surrender! I surrender! Please don't kill me!"

He slows down his horse and climbs down. He raises his sword and brings it to my shoulder. He dangles it in front of my neck. I feel the coldness of the tip against my Adam's apple. The smell of blood is ripe as it dripped onto my clothes.

"Wat' you say?" The nigger asks me.

"I say I give up! Please don't kill me!" I repeat loudly. Looking around, I garner the attention of all the negroes. The only white left around to hear my surrender is the Commander.

"Never give up! Especially to some niggers!" Commander yells at me with disdain in his eyes.

It's inconceivable that I, a white man, would consider kneeling, in the presence of some niggers, who's place is among the animals. However, that proves to be his mistake. Due to him focusing on what I'm doing, he creates an opening for one of those eight niggers to take him to the ground. Knocking loose his sword. The rest jump on him.

We have failed.
Jerusalem has fallen to the hands of the niggers
The only question, as this bloodied blade rests near my neck,
Will I too, fall? I ask myself.

25

God is on Our Side - Tues. Aug 23, 1831 07:00 AM

"Don't move, boy!" I shout while holdin' my sword to his throat.

It be amazin' wat' time will do. I ain't think me, Reagor, would get to call a white man a boy and live.

I ain't never had no power like 'dis here! A person's life endin' or livin' is at my fingers.

'Till today.

"Tie 'em both up! Let Nat decide wat' to do wit' 'em." Will shouts at those standin' 'round.

I turn to look at him and see he's holdin' his left arm covered in blood.

"You okay?" I ask.

"I'll be fine. Keep 'em steady 'til they come to tie his hands and feet." Will responds.

Four men come ova' wit' some hangin' rope and tie up the boy's hands and feet. While they tie him, I was watchin' him close.

Somethin' 'bout 'em is familiar.

The eight surroundin' the Commander drag him ova' and put him alongside the boy. They rest in the middle of the enclosed armory. Slain bodies are layin' up and down the compound. Outside the gates, no help can be found for these white boys. Just as Nat dreamed, we done taken control of Jerusalem!

The black soldiers that be outside start comin' inside the armory eyin' the two last white men. I stand in front as I watch the circle grow bigger and bigger up 'round them. Just like everybody up in there, 'dey wanna' see the look on they faces that this be group of negroes 'dat done took they town from 'em.

No one speaks. The Commander steady strugglin' to get up from bein' face down in the dirt. It's hard keepin' from laughin' just watchin' him rollin' 'round like a beheaded chicken. Once he finally get to his knees and see his audience, he starts runnin' off at the mouth.

"Y'all some dead niggers come morning! You hear me!? What makes you think you can come up through here and have the audacity to slay these fine white men, women, and chilren'! Oh, I can't wait 'til they come and free me. We are gonna' rangle y'all niggers up like never before! Oh, it won't be any merciful deaths given to any of you. We gonna' take our time with y'all! I'm gonna' see to it that y'all suffer under the full extent of the law, and y'all receive your just punishment in this life before we send ya' ova' to receive ya' eternal punishment from the Good Lord himself!"

"Is that so?!" was shouted.

From the back, you see the Black Sea part. Nat be comin' up to see wats waitin' for him up front.

He walks to the front to speak wit' the Commander face to face. First, he hands me his hatchet before he takin' a deep breath. He then gives the Commander his attention.

Wit' one foot followin' the other, Nat gets ungodly close to the Commander. He so close on the Commander, the Commander gotta' lift his head up to see Nat's face. A few seconds pass 'fore Nat falls to one knee to be at eye level.

"Sir, I don't think you understand. The Good Lord sent me and 'dis army. See, you and ya' kindred have made a disgrace of ya'selves. You've raped, stolen, found pleasure in evil and bloodshed of many people. God has judged y'all guilty for crimes against His creation. At this perfect time, he has unleashed us to harbor his justice."

"We are that justice."

The Commander bursts out laughin'. His loud laugh runs through the camp for all to hear. Once he settles down, all falls quiet. Lookin' Nat in the eye, he does the unthinkable. He spits in Nat's face.

"Wat' the hell you doin' lookin' me in the eye, boy! Don't you ever in ya' life think you can disrespect me by lookin' me in the face. You ain't nothin' but a fuckin' nigger! Here to do whatever we tell you to do! You, these boys and girls 'round here ain't nothin' but whatever WE say you are! You live because WE say you can live. Don't you dare look me in the eye, boy! Show me some damn respect!"

Crouchin' on one knee, Nat hangs his face low as he gets back to his feet. He slowly lifts his head for all to see wat' 'dis man did to his face.

You feel the weight of the quiet in 'dis moment.

Pigs do everythin' in they own stank, yet I've seen a white man respect and love on 'em. A white man never found a pig worthless 'nuff to spit on 'em. This white man find it in the depths of his tar black heart and soul to spit in Nat's face. If ya' Massa' ever spit on ya', you knew death was near 'cus he thinks of ya' to be less than dirt.

I'm sure even the Lord himself was waitin' for Nat's response.

Nat wipes the thick spit slidin' down his eyelid and lip off wit' the bottom of his shirt. He walks ova' to the Commander to stand tall ova' 'em.

"Reagor?"

"Sir?"

"Grab three men."

"Dig a hole."

26
Make it a Home - Tues. Aug 23, 1831 07:20 AM

"CLINK- CLINK...THWACK! CLINK - CLINK... THWACK!"

"CLINK- CLINK...THWACK! CLINK - CLINK... THWACK!"

"CLINK- CLINK...THWACK! CLINK - CLINK... THWACK!"

Be the rhythm of shovels diggin' in the ground and tossin' dirt aside. The four of us keeps diggin' deeper and wider behind the white men. Nat is stubborn 'bout it bein' just one. The more we dig, the more we have to keep pushin' people up out the way. They is dyin' to see wat's gonna' happen.

The whole time we diggin', Nat stands tall ova' the Commander, never restin' his eyes on anythin' but him. The Commander wasn't breakin' his stare either.

"Sir. The hole is dug." I report lookin' for my second wind.

"Good. Stand 'em up."

"Bind his hands in front of him."

"Bind his feet tighter."

"Now... Bury him up to his shoulders!"
A hush fell ova' Jerusalem.

"CLINK- CLINK...THWACK! CLINK - CLINK... THWACK!"
"CLINK- CLINK...THWACK! CLINK - CLINK... THWACK!"

Went the dirt seepin' in all 'round him. We keep packin' it down tighter and tighter leavin' nuff room for 'em to keep breathin'. The Commander stayed still, never brakin' his face for nothin'. After we burryin' him and made sho' he was tight in 'dat hole. Nat crouches back down to one knee and begins to give his talk fo' the hole to the Commander and us watchin'.

"You see, I'm not gonna' kill you. Despite wat' you may be thinkin', I don't wanna kill any of ya'. But wat' I won't allow, is for you and ya' people to keep strippin' everythin' from us."

"Our humanity, our manhood, our women, our families, our right to live and exist wit'out fear! See, you don't know wat' it's like to see ya' child taken from ya' and expect to wear a smile knowin' ya' failed to protect ya' family. Or be stripped naked, whipped, and have salt poured in ya' wounds for laughter. Or have ya' wife look at ya' wit' tears across the room while ya' held up wit' a riffle at ya' neck watchin' her bein' raped ova' and ova' again. Beggin' for ya' to save her and wit' all ya' strength, you can't do nothin' to save her."

"Y'all have succeeded in breakin' us down to the dirt we came from. But at this moment, we have the victory that will aid us in restorin' ourselves. 'Dis here is where we stand. Where we will heal, come together, move onward. Just like when God breathed into Adam, 'dis here is where we will breathe life into one another! 'Dis here is where men will become men, our women will be able to be women, our chil'ren will be chil'ren. We will take nothin' less."

"You... you will be the first of ya' people to see it all. You will see us train, work, watch us unshackle ourselves from the comforts of the chains placed on us so we can unify. It's high time we find comfort in freedom. You'll watch us grow as one! I won't have a reason to kill ya'. Ya' hatred in ya' heart, the lies ya' found joy and purpose in, will eat ya' alive. Ya' won't be able to tolerate wat' ya' see. Ya' helplessness will consume ya'. For ya' wickedness will have nowhere to go. Unless ya' decide to change. We will feed ya', give ya' water, and keep ya' healthy. And when the Lord deems us strong 'nuff, we will let ya' go for you sir gonna' be a disciple for the good news of wat' ya' done seen.

Nat gets to his feet this time wit' no spit found on his face. His eyes look ova' the dozens of beautiful faces of men and women that moved in faith to follow.

"Wat' say you?!"

A monstrous response from the victors rose to glory wit', "Yeah!"

Nat grows a smile on his face as he stands in 'dis special moment. A glimma' begin growin' in the eyes of the people that be somethin' to behold.

At 'dis moment, even in my heart, I could feel a rumble of somethin'. Beneath the terribleness of sufferin', somethin' starts diggin' it's way out.

A restoration of Hope.

As all quiets, I call on Nat,

"Sir?"

"Yeah?"

"Wat' of 'dis one?"

"Where be ya' jail?" Nat asks the young white man.

"It's... It's down at the end. To the right, before you get to the stables... Sir,"

"Place him in there and we shall pray on it. No one will kill this lad." Nat commands.

"Yessir."

"Get 'em up!" I command two of the men next to him. They pull 'em up and we begin marchin' to the back. I keep my presence known pushin' my blade in his back.

As we walk to the back we come to a locked door.

"Where 'dem keys?!"

He swing his hands up, "they're right there. On the side hangin' up."

I look up and down the wall to find 'em. They be five keys on 'em.

"Which one?"

"The second, I think..." He says sadly.

As I place the key in the lock, I stand ready wit' my sword. I hear the click of the lock and swing the door open. A cold gust of wind leaves the room, but no one came rushin' out, so I think it be safe.

I slowly step into the room and find inside a black woman strung up high in the air. Naked wit' ropes at her wrists and her feet. It keep her hangin' high in the air like the bell on Massa' Mills tower fo' all to see. Lash marks slain all ova' her back. On the other side be a white man strung up high and naked too. He got whippins' goin' 'cross his back too. The smell in the room is worse than a pigpen.

"Wat' in the world..." I mumble out steppin' in the room.

I slowly stick my sword out and touch her side soft 'til her body jerks. By grace, she still be alive. The lady's arms start movin' while she's wakin' up. She lifts her heavy crown towards the door where we see her face be swollen on one side. Wit' her good eye she able to find me and flashes a smile. She looks 'cross the room at the white man and musters up the strength to talk,

211

"Hey! Will— William... looka' here! Hell musta' froze ova' 'cus 'dey be some negroes holdin' swords at the door!"

He too brings his head ova' then looks back at the woman. We hear 'em chuckle through they lingerin' pain.

I angrily turn and shovin' the white boy on the floor restin' my sword at his neck,

"Why they strung up like 'dis here?!"

Shakin' on the floor, he tries to turn from me to answer, "Please! They were just some prisoners! I didn't hurt them. All I did was watch them and keep them alive!"

I shout at the two wit' me, "Set 'em loose! Get 'em ova' to Nat. String his ass up there!"

Aug 23, 1831 09:00 AM: County Jail, Jerusalem VA

'Cross the way from the armory be the county jail. It sits at a prime place to see a side of the boundary to the town. Nat thought it best to meet there and the prisoners join us to learn of 'em.

"So, you tellin' me that the time I been strung up there like a piece of meat some negroes been comin' up through Virginia just settin' the captives free?!" The lady wrapped up in blankets asks.

"Yessum'. I believe it was the work of the Lord, so I just let 'em use me. And these brave people came along." Nat answers her.

She start laughin', "Don't tell me prayer don't change thangs! Course we been prayin' fo' some time now!"

The room joins in on the laugh— much needed laugh fo' all us.

"So before we go any further, we gotta' know who and why was y'all strung up and locked away." Nat asks.

"Well, my name be Sojourner Truth 'cus I speak the truth as the Holy Spirit see fit to work in me. They thought that I be a runaway, but I'm not. I'm a free woman. Due to my kind looks, it's kinda' hard to slip through wit'out eyes lookin' at ya."

I thought to myself, she was tellin' the truth. This lady was as tall as two of me wit' da' hands to match. She seems like she'd be a field hand since ya' see all the bruises and hardness on her.

"I got some friends up North but came down South to speak 'bout the hell of slavery and it needin' to end. I didn't get a chance to make it to where I needed to be. God willin' kept me alive, though!"

Turnin' ova' to the white man wit' the glasses, Nat asks him who he be.

"My name is William Lloyd Garrison. I'm from Boston, Massachusetts. I'm a member of an abolition movement up North and founder of an abolitionist newspaper in which I expose the hell that is slavery, white Christian contradictions, and implore whites to join the movement of putting an end to slavery. Some whites who are not fond of my message spotted me in Baltimore delivering a speech. I was incarcerated for six months before releasing me for lack of evidence. I knew it was because of my speech and condemnation I spoke with towards whites. After my time, I felt a tug on my spirit to travel further down South. So I did so to gather information for my paper and expose the evil here in the epicenter. I went to South Carolina and was exposed again. Once I saw there was a bounty for my life, I traveled quickly to Virginia. I thought I wouldn't be recognized here in Jerusalem given its distance. I was sadly mistaken. The Sheriff and Commander thought it best to lock me away for some time to break me of my, "nigger loving affection.""

"Yeah, that didn't work all too well 'cus they locked him up wit' me, and we been gettin' along just fine!" Sojourner shouts out.

"Well thank ya' for ya' stories."

"Now that we took ova' Jerusalem, Nat, wat's next? Ya' know they gonna' be comin' for us wit' more weapons than ever." Hark says to get the focus back.

"Yes, yes, I know. We must be smart wit' our time. We must set up protection 'round wat's ours."

"Wait, so y'all stayin'?" Sojourner asks.

"We doin' more than that! We gonna' free more to join us. We not gonna' stop here. I don't know wat' we gonna' do yet, but we must do somethin'."

All fell silent wit' no ideas.

He's right, we gotta' do somethin'. I didn't wanna go through all 'dis just to get killed at the end.

"Well... if you feel the Lawd done told ya' to set up here, do it. He won't steer ya' wrong, no sir!" Sojourner preachin' out loud. You can tell she loves her Lawd.

"You think ya' can get me headed back up North?" Sojourner asks.

"If ya' can keep alive long 'nuff I can go back up North and do wat' I can to help ya' wit' my friends. My white friends."

"We sho' nuff can get ya' where ya' need to be." Hark says strongly.

Nudgin' William next to her, "Wat' say you, William?! You a white friend of mine, right?"

Securin' his glasses on his face, "Yes. I believe I can provide some strong assistance if I can get back home. I have allies and my paper is known well amongst the free black communities up North. If we plan correctly, you can have some help quickly. A question I have is how many are with you?"

Nat looks up at me. I say, "Before the fight, they was one - three-seven. I can go out and count again?"

"Well, if you have anything close to that, don't underestimate your strength as a group. Continue to lead them. I'll offer my help anyway I can as long as it's to abolish slavery." William says calmly.

Nat stands from the table and starts pacin'.

"We have in our hands a town wit' a mercantile store, hotel, doctor's house, and carriage maker. If we come together as one we can make 'dis here last! Let's go forth wit' haste. Waste no time, we gotta' work."

As everyone starts to leave I see Nat signal to me. I await until the room is him and I.

"I wanted to let ya' know you did a great job today!" Nat says lookin' at me eye to eye wit' a proud smile.

"Thank ya' sir. I'm glad I played a role."

"You done more 'den a role wit' us here. You have a place and a purpose. Don't forget 'dat, for as moments come, failure from 'dis point forward can't happen."

I nod my head while tryna' grasp all 'dat he is layin' on me.

"Shall I go count?" I ask tryna' leave the room.

"Before you do, take 'dis here wit' ya'." Nat slings his satchel up on the table.

"Keep usin' 'dis here for practicin' ya' readin'. I need ya' to be just as good as you be wit' 'dem numbers."

Graspin' the bag off the table, "Yes Sir. I be sho' to practice everyday."

"Be sho' 'dat you do. Watever you may need, just come get me and I'll be here for ya'."

27

RESTORATION CELEBRATION

Aug 23, 1831 01:10 PM: Mayor James Trezevant's Office

"Them dirty niggers," Mayor Trezevant utters while pouring General Broadnax a scotch.

They both hold up glasses to which they toast.

"Yes Sir, I agree with ya'. They made quite a mess down there. Yet my men and I succeeded in taking back control. You won't have any more problems with the niggers left."

The Mayor and General walk to take seats,

"What do you mean?"

"Let's just say we left a fleshly reminder of why you shouldn't mess with the system in place. Don't worry. We brought all the leaders back in one piece and some others so the Governor can have his moment with the people."

"Mhhm," Mayor Trezevant says after taking a hefty sip of his premium whiskey.

"Was that other nigger boy still down there when you locked up the rest?"

"Yessir."

"Good. Maybe he will start to confess, being we caught all his co-conspirators. These niggers think they so smart when they don't have the ability to think as we do. I don't know why it's so hard for them to accept their role. Life for everyone would be glorious. They are trying to destroy this utopian opportunity given to us."

"Well, they all will definitely think twice about that now. I'm sure as word grows, the free ones won't want to stay around."

"Good, we can also put a stop to this panic of this being a British attack."

"Hey Thomas!" Mayor Trezevant shouts.

"Yes Sir?"

"Draft up a letter quickly to Governor Floyd for me to sign, please. Let him know the state militia of 3,500 men is no longer required. We have successfully stopped the insurrection."

"Yes Sir, right away."

"To the South!" Mayor Trezevant shouts while raising his glass.

"To the South, forever the Lord shall show favor upon us!" General Broadnax says while raising his glass.

November 26, 2016 02:15 AM: Whitfield Living Room

"Nessa...Vanessa...Vanessa!"

"Huh? Where am I?"

"You fell asleep on the couch, girl. It's two in the morning. You're supposed to be in bed."

Wiping my eyes, trying to comprehend what's happening,

"Yeah... I was just busy working on something."

As dad helps me to my feet he responds, "Yeah, I know I saw it. There will be time for that later, just go to bed now, 'aight?"

Walking away, in the twilight zone, I stumble towards the stairs saying, "Sure thing... Goodnight."

"Goodnight."

As I make my way up, Dad comes around the corner behind me,

"Hey 'Nessa?"

"Yeah?"

"Did... did you write all that on your own?"

"... Yup."

"So... what happens next?"

As I rub my eyes, I sober up a little.

"They go to work. Goodnight Dad."

BIBLIOGRAPHY

1. "A Clever Hero: Slave Revolt Leader Charles Deslondes." Interview by

    Guy Raz. *Tell Me More,* 11 Feb. 2011,

    https://www.npr.org/2011/02/11/133684831/A-

    Tribute-To-Slave-Revolt-Leader-Charles-Deslonde. Accessd

    21 Aug. 2020.

2. "Africans in America/Part 3/Nat Turner's Rebellion." *PBS*, PBS,

    www.pbs.org/wgbh/aia/part3/3p1518.html. Accessed 11 Jul.

    2020.

3. Britannica, The Editors of Encyclopaedia. "Denmark Vesey."

    Encyclopedia Britannica, 28 Jun. 2020,

    https://www.britannica.com/biography/Denmark-Vesey.

    Accessed 29 Jun. 2020.

4. Britannica, The Editors of Encyclopaedia. "Gabriel." *Encyclopedia*

    Britannica, 28 Aug. 2020,

https://www.britannica.com/biography/Gabriel-American-

bondsman. Accessed 29 Jun. 2020.

5. Britannica, The Editors of Encyclopaedia. "Great Dismal Swamp."

    Encyclopedia Britannica, 16 Apr. 2018,

    https://www.britannica.com/place/Great-Dismal-Swamp.

    Accessed 10 Jul. 2020.

6. Britannica, The Editors of Encyclopaedia. "Nat Turner." *Encyclopedia

    Britannica*, 17 May 2018,

    https://www.britannica.com/biography/Nat-Turner.

    Accessed 10 Jul. 2020.

7. Cain, William E., ed. *William Lloyd Garrison and the Fight Against

    Slavery: Selections from The Liberator*. Boston: Bedford Books

    of St. Martin's Press, 1995.

8. "Compassion." *YouTube*, uploaded by BibleProject, 1 Sept. 2020,

    www.youtube.com/watch?v=qJEtyAiAQik. Accessed 28 May

    2020.

9. "Death or Liberty." *Nat Turner's Rebellion*,

    www.lva.virginia.gov/exhibits/DeathLiberty

    /natturner/index.htm. Accessed 23 Aug. 2020.

10. Edwards, Frank. "Risk of Being Killed by Police Use of Force in the United States by Age, Race–Ethnicity, and Sex." *PNAS*, 20 Aug. 2019, www.pnas.org/content/116/34/16793. Accessed 19 Sep. 2020.

11. Erikson, Mark St. John. "Remembering the Horror of Nat Turner's Rebellion on This Day in 1831." *Daily Press*, 21 Aug. 2018, www.tribpub.com/gdpr/dailypress.com. Accessed 11 Jul. 2020.

12. Focus on the Family, and Lysa TerKeurst. "Embracing Messy, Beautiful Forgiveness (Part 1) - Lysa TerKeurst." *YouTube*, uploaded by Focus on the Family, 17 Nov. 2020, www.youtube.com/watch?v=ePOqPscKDNs. Accessed 05 Sep. 2020.

13. Francis, Richard. Interview. Conducted by Charles Price, 17 Dec. 2020.

14. Francis, Richard. Interview. Conducted by Charles Price, 22 Jan. 2021.

15. Freehling, Allison. "Brodnax, William H. (ca. 1786–1834)." *Encyclopedia Virginia.* Virginia Humanities, (12 Feb. 2019).

16. French, Scot. *The Rebellious Slave: Nat Turner in American Memory.*

    First Edition, Houghton Mifflin Company, 2004.

17. "Gabriel's Conspiracy." *Africans In America*, PBS/WETA,

    www.pbs.org/wgbh/aia/part3/3p1576.html. Accessed 22 Jun.

    2020.

18. Higginson, Thomas Wentworth. "Nat Turner's Insurrection." *The*

    Atlantic, Aug. 1861, www.theatlantic.com/magazine/archive/

    1861/08/nat-turners-insurrection/308736. Accessed 24 May

    2020.

19. "TREZVANT, James." History, Art & Archives, U.S. House of

    Representatives, https://history.house.gov/People/Listing/

    T/TREZVANT,-James-(T000365). Accessed 15 Aug. 2020.

20. Holt, C. Thomas, and Brown, B. Elsa. *Major Problems in African -*

    American History Volume I: From Slavery to Freedom,

    1619-1877. Houghton Mifflin Company, 2000.

21. Hotchkiss, Jedediah. Sussex, Southampton counties, *Virginia. 1867.*

    Map. Retrieved from the Library of Congress,

    <www.loc.gov/item/2005625191/>. Accessed 03 Jun. 2020

22. Kestenbaum, Lawrence. "The Political Graveyard." *Southampton County Virginia*, 19 Aug. 2019,

politicalgraveyard.com/geo/VA/SO.html#BORN.

23. Lynch, Hollis. "African Americans." *Encyclopedia Britannica*,

17 Aug. 2020, https://www.britannica.com/topic/

African-American. Accessed 18 June 2020.

24. "NAT TURNER: A Troublesome Property. Nat Turner | PBS."

Independent Lens, PBS, www.pbs.org/independentlens/

natturner/nat.html. Accessed 17 July 2020.

25. "Path of Nat Turner's Rebellion." *StoryMapJS*,

uploads.knightlab.com/storymapjs/

a22728634385fc4958eefc346a6d888c/path-of-nat-

turners-rebellion/index.html. Accessed 21 Aug. 2020.

26. Perry, Jackie-Hill. "No Ways Tired feat. Joseph Solomn." *Crescendo*,

Humble Beast, 2018, https://store.humblebeast.com/

products/crescendo-cd-jackie-hill-perry.

27. Pope-Levison, Priscilla. "Sojourner Truth (ca. 1797-1883)." *BlackPast*,

20 Nov. 2020,

www.blackpast.org/african-american-history/truth-sojourner-isabella-baumfree-ca-1797-1883. Accessed 17 Aug. 2020.

28. Rae, Noel. "How Christian Slaveholders Used the Bible to Justify Slavery." *Time*, 23 Feb. 2018, www.time.com/5171819/ christianity-slavery-book-excerpt. Accessed 18 Aug. 2020.

29. Ramsden, Michael. "What Is Love? | Michael Ramsden." *YouTube*, uploaded by HTB Church, 1 Oct. 2018, www.youtube.com/watch?v=JQGss4R8HSk.

30. Rasmussen, Daniel. "American Rising: When Slaves Attacked New Orleans." Interview by Guy Raz. *All Things Considered*, 16 Jan. 2011, https://www.npr.org/2011/01/16/132839717/ american-rising-when-slaves-took-on-new-orleans. Accessed 19 Jun. 2020.

31. Rasmussen, Daniel. *American Uprising: The Untold Story of America's Largest Slave Revolt*. Harper Perennial, 2012.

32. Reed, Wilson Edward. "Nat Turner (1800-1831)." *Black Past*, 12 Feb. 2007, www.blackpast.org/african-american-history/ turner-nat-1800-1831. Accessed 10 Jul. 2020.

33. Schmidt, Anthony. "Slave Bible From The 1800s Omitted Key

   Passages That Could Incite Rebellion." Interview by Michel

   Martin. *All Things Considered,* 09 Dec. 2018,

   https://www.npr.org/2018/12/09/674995075/slave-bible-

   from-the-1800s-omitted-key-passages-that-could

   -incite-rebellion. Accessed 19 Jun. 2020.

34. "Seeds of Conflict: The Beanbody Histories—The Civil War." *Just for*

   Kids, Films Media Group, 2015, jfk.infobase.com/

   PortalPlaylists.aspx?wID=12190&xtid=107885. Accessed 29

   Jul. 2020.

35. "Slavery and the Making of America: The Slave Experience: Men,

   Women & Gender | PBS." *Slavery and the Making of*

   America, Thirteen/WNET New York,

   www.thirteen.org/wnet/slavery/experience/gender/

   feature6.html. Accessed 11 Aug. 2020.

36. "S2E10: What Is BIBLICAL JUSTICE and How Can We Achieve It?

   W/ Rev. A.R. Bernard." *YouTube*, uploaded by Cross

   Examined, 30 Sept. 2020,

www.youtube.com/watch?v=N32kjBAPjB8. Accessed 04 Jul. 2020.

37. *The Black Church: This Is Our Story, This Is Our Song.* Produced by Louis Gates, Jr., McGee Media, Inkwell Media, and WETA Washington, D.C. 2021.

38. *The Bible.* Authorized King James Version, Oxford UP, 1998.

39. "This Far by Faith: Denmark Vesey | PBS." *This Far By Faith*, The Faith Project/PBS/WETA, www.pbs.org/thisfarbyfaith/people/denmark_vesey.html. Accessed 12 Jun. 2020.

40. Thomas, John. "William Lloyd Garrison | Biography & Facts." *Encyclopedia Britannica*, Britannica, 20 May 2020, www.britannica.com/biography/William-Lloyd-Garrison. Accessed 29 Jul. 2020.

41. Truth, Sojourner, and Margaret Washington. *Narrative of Sojourner Truth.* 1st ed., Vintage Classics Original, 1993.

42. Turner, Nat, 1800?-1831, and Thomas R Gray. *The confessions of Nat Turner, the leader of the late insurrection in Southampton, Va. as fully, &etc.* Richmond, T. R. Gray, 1832. Pdf.

Retrieved from the Library of Congress,

<www.loc.gov/item/07009643/>. Accessed 19 May 2020.

43. Ushistory.org. "Gabriel's Rebellion: Another View of Virginia in

1800." *U.S. History Online Textbook*, U.S. History Online

Textbook, 1 Jan. 2020.

44. "Virginia Memory - This Day in Virginia History." *Virginia Memory:

Library of Virginia*, www.virginiamemory.com/reading_room

/this_day_in_virginia_history/october/31. Accessed 15 Aug.

2020.

45. Waxman, Olivia. "The Most Important Slave Revolt That Never

Happened." *Time*, Time Magazine, 15 Mar. 2017,

time.com/4701283/denmark-vesey-history-charleston-

south-carolina. Accessed 06 Jul. 2020.

46. Wilkerson, Isabel. *Caste: The Origins of Our Discontents*. 1st ed.,

Random House, 2020.

47. "William Lloyd Garrison." *PBS*, WETA,

www.pbs.org/wgbh/aia/part4/4p1561.html. Accessed 29 Jul.

2020.

ABOUT THE AUTHOR
VISIT US!

TWITTER: @THECOUNCIL_BOOK
WEBSITE: WWW.COUNCILSERIES.COM
EMAIL: THECOUNCILSERIES016@GMAIL.COM

Description: 31 years old. Resides in Northern VA. Joyfully married. Fearfully and wonderfully made, dipped in dark chocolate, with some awesome sauce on the side.

Likes: Movies, books, TV, God, skydiving, science, family, the gym, making friends, The Eagles (Fly, Eagles, Fly!), and jazz/ chillhop

Dislikes: Conflict, Caramel, War, laziness, strange foods, cancel culture, politics, greed, simplification of humanity, baseball (sorry just not a fan LOL)

Strengths: Compassion, meekness, humor, willingness to push myself, having difficult conversations, resolve, ability to love and show it, telling the truth, strong in mind, body, and spirit.

Weakness: Taking harsh and honest criticism, trying weird foods

Fears: God, my ego, my vanity, not living up to my potential and intent

Favorite Quotes: "When you want to succeed as bad as you wanna breathe then you will be successful." - Eric Thomas

"Stay focused on your divine purpose." - Charles Price II

Biggest Dreams:

1. I'm in line at Chipotle, and I pay for my burrito. The sales rep looks at me and pauses. They say, "Hey, aren't you that guy that did that thing?" to which I reply, "Yup." Then I just walk out.

2. Taking fifty kids that have succeeded academically and fifty other kids who have dramatically turned their life around in challenging communities along with their parents to Barcelona. Show a sense of pride, joy, and thankfulness as we watch the sunrise ova' Parc Güell. Everyone should get to experience a life-changing sunrise.